Ruff-Housed

Susan J. Kroupa

LAUREL FORK PRESS

Published by Laurel Fork Press
Laurel Fork, Virginia
www.laurelforkpress.com

Photo and Cover Credits:
Labradoodle: © 2016 by Joseph A. Kroupa
White House: © 2016 by Joseph A. Kroupa
Protest signs: 2jenn/Shutterstock.com
Cover by Keri Knutson, Alchemy Book Covers and Design
Book Design by Marny K. Parkin

In memory of Sarah Anne Phoebe Dunaway

Books by Susan J. Kroupa

The Doodlebugged Mysteries

Bed-Bugged

Out-Sniffed

Dog-Nabbed

Bad-Mouthed

Ruff-Housed

Contents

How It All Began   7

Dog Fight   11

Dog Days   23

Another Surprise   33

HEAR   41

Tanya   49

Good Citizen   61

Hershey   67

Blind Dan   79

Uncle Armando's Surprise   87

Breaking the Law   99

Proof!   109

Eyewitness   115

Mr. Blevins   123

Caught in the Act	131
Awkward Conversations	141
Meeting the Family	147
Silvia	155
Annie	165
Demonstration	173
Drop Off	187
Explanations	199
An Unhappy Discovery	209
Confrontation	217
Happier Times	227
Moving On	237
About the Author	241
Acknowledgements	243

Chapter 1

How It All Began

HERE'S THE STORY OF WHAT HAPPENED WHEN I TOOK the Canine Good Citizen test. Actually, it is the story of a bunch of other things, too, but they all mostly started with the test, which Molly says turned out to be way more complicated, not to mention dangerous, than she planned.

The idea to take the test came from Molly's friend, Grady, who goes to her school, but is in a different class. She met Grady when his mother did this big video blog about the bed-bug business that the boss (Molly's dad) and I run—he gets the jobs, I sniff out the bugs.

The blog had tons of what the boss calls "unintended consequences." Not sure what he means, except he went from texting and calling Grady's mother all day, to being really angry with her for a while. In fact, things got pretty exciting all around. That's when, as Molly puts it, "Grady saved our bacon," which can only be a good thing, right? Although, to be honest, I don't actually remember any bacon being involved, which is strange because bacon is something I don't usually forget.

What I do remember is that Grady ended up adopting Snippet, a dog he calls a "Golden Irish mix," and that changed everything. Grady quit talking about moving back to Alabama to live with his dad. He started taking Snippet on walks and playing ball with her. And he started to get interested in dog training.

Anyway, Grady heard about the Canine Good Citizen certification test, which, let me tell you, turns out to be way easier to pass than the scent-detection test I have to take for my job with the boss. And he suggested that Molly and I could train with him and Snippet to take the test, since Molly knows a bunch more about dog training than he does.

So Molly goes to the boss. "Please?" she asks, her brown eyes wide with pleading, much like Snippet's when she's begging for a treat. "It'll be good for the business. You could tell our customers Doodle is a Canine Good Citizen."

The boss gives her a slightly exasperated look. "No one has asked so far. And, anyway, are you sure he doesn't already have it? With all his training . . ."

"He doesn't. I called Annie, and she said that she and Miguel don't do those certifications, and when they adopted him and checked his microchip and researched him, there was no record that he ever got the CGC."

Annie is a great friend to Molly and me and especially to the boss, who is always texting her (except for that short time when he was texting Grady's mom.) Annie trains dogs and works for Miguel, the man who taught me to be a bed-bug dog.

The boss frowns and rubs his beard. "Who runs this? The American Kennel Club?"

Molly nods.

"Will they take labradoodles? Mixed breeds?"

Another nod. "Any dog can take the CGC," she says. "Even mutts like Doodle." She says this with affection, stroking me under my chin. She likes to tell me that we're both mutts, me because I'm a Labrador retriever/poodle mix, and her because, in her words, "Mom is Mexican-American and Dad is Irish-American, so I'm kind of a human labradoodle."

She continues, still in a pleading tone, "And I can help Grady train Snippet since I've had classes with Annie." When the boss doesn't respond, she adds, "And if we went on and Doodle could pass the advanced test—the Canine Good Citizen Community— then he'd be eligible to go into rest homes as a therapy dog."

"Doodle?" The boss snorts. "What kind of therapy? Shock therapy?" He laughs, pleased with himself. "Shock therapy. That's a good one. Right, Doodle?"

I wag my tail, not sure what he's talking about.

But Molly doesn't so much as crack a smile. "Doodle's good with people. All the kids in my class love him."

"Little do they know," the boss says, but he's still smiling. He's been in a good mood lately because we've had lots of work. One of his favorite sayings is "work means money" because money means he can pay the rent, which the boss claims is "sky high" here in Arlington where we live. Don't quite get the sky connection, but he means it costs a lot to live here. The boss worries about money all the time. The only thing he worries about more is traffic, something that's always on his mind. Well, and Molly, of course.

"I guess it'll be okay. Of course, when I have work, I'll need Doodle with me."

I'll say. The only way he'd find bed bugs without my nose would be if they all decided to rush out from their hiding places to greet him. Don't think that's going to happen.

Chapter 2

Dog Fight

HEY, WHAT'S THAT GUY DOING ON OUR LAWN?" GRADY peers out his living room window and runs a hand through his short, straight-up hair.

A man wearing a baseball hat and an overweight, blocky-faced dog, some kind of boxer/pit bull mix, are in the front yard. The dog is squatting in a way that leaves no question as to what it's doing. The dog wears a giant prong collar round its neck, attached to a thick leather leash. The man holding the leash is dressed in plaid shorts that come down almost to his knee, and a windbreaker, open to show a bright knit shirt that rounds over his belly.

"Maybe he doesn't know you're living here," Molly suggests. "Since it's only been a few days."

In fact, that's why Molly and I are here. Grady and his mother, Madison, just moved into this house and Grady wanted Molly to see it, so Madison picked us up after Molly got home from school, and the boss said he'd come get us before dinner.

"If he doesn't know we're here, we need to tell him," Grady says, still staring out the window. "How rude to use someone else's yard."

He grabs a leash on a table near the door while Molly goes to her backpack, which she dropped in front of the door when we first came in. She bends down and unzips it, but bumps the door just as she's pulling out my leash. The door must not have been closed all the way, because it swings open. Snippet sticks her head out, sees the dog, and squeezes through the opening before Molly can close it.

"Snippet, no!" Molly chases after her, hand outstretched to grab her collar.

Snippet hesitates for a second, taking in the man and the dog, her nose working, her ears forward with curiosity. A second before Molly reaches her she bolts forward, towards the man and the dog.

Uh-oh.

Here's the thing. Snippet is optimistic in the way that golden retrievers and setters tend to be, assuming that because they love everyone, everyone loves them back. Labs can be that way, too, all happy-go-lucky, oblivious to body language. But, I might have mentioned before that even though I'm a labradoodle, my looks and personality strongly favor the poodle side of the mix. Poodles are friendly, to be sure. We're not perpetually grumpy like, say, chows, or yappy like a lot of small dogs, or suspicious like many of the breeds of watch dogs. But we're smart enough to read body language. And this boxer/pit's body language shouts CAUTION!

Snippet isn't cautious. She barrels full speed towards the dog, who gives her an apprehensive look and then flattens his ears and lowers his head.

There's going to be trouble. I lunge forward, to the sound of Molly shouting, "Doodle, no!"

Snippet skids up to dog, tail wagging, her mouth soft with happiness, clueless about the dog's body language. He attacks, snarling and biting. I rush in to break things up. Can't let Snippet get hurt. And this intruder needs a lesson. What kind of dog attacks another on that dog's own property? I mean, seriously? He needs to respect Snippet's territory.

These kinds of scuffles are usually all noise and snapping in a way that no one gets hurt, but this boxer/pit is biting harder than normal. I hear Molly yell my name, and then Grady races towards us, shouting, "SNIPPET!" Snippet hesitates, glancing at him. The boxer/pit snaps at her neck as she turns toward Grady. I don't think so! I push between him and Snippet, and he snaps wildly several times, just as the man tries to seize his collar.

"Ow!" The boxer/pit's owner yells, flinging back his hand. He tries to land a kick on Snippet, but she's already on her way to Grady, which means my job is done. I jump back and head for Molly. She grabs my collar. Whoa. She's really angry and I can feel her hands trembling as she snaps on the leash. Grady's doing the same thing with Snippet.

"They bit me," he screams. "Your—" here, he uses what the boss calls "language"—"dogs bit me."

What? Snippet's head was turned away, and I'm certain my teeth didn't touch human flesh. A bit of pit bull skin, yes, but nothing else.

Both Grady and Molly are stammering apologies. "I'm so sorry." Molly looks near tears.

"Snippet has never bitten anyone," Grady says, white-faced. "She's super friendly."

"Friendly?" The man's eyes bulge, his expression incredulous. He smells like stale sweat and beer, which makes sense because he has what the boss calls a beer belly. He's wearing thick-soled white athletic shoes, although with his fat belly and skinny (though hairy) legs he doesn't look much like an athlete. "These are vicious dogs. They ought to be put down. I'm going to call Animal Control and get them taken away."

"What?" Molly stares at the man in disbelief, her eyes wide with shock. "No one was hurt."

"No one hurt?" he yells. "Your—" more language—"dog bit me, you stupid—" he uses a word that isn't language when talking about female dogs, but, for reasons unknown to me, is considered insulting to humans.

He jabs a finger at her, a vicious motion that makes me growl.

"Doodle!" Molly whispers in anguish.

"See what I mean?" The man repeats the gesture. "That dog's a menace. Both of them are. They ran out and attacked us."

"Don't talk to her that way." Grady steps forward, coming between Molly and the man.

"Watch it, or I'll have you arrested for assault." The man, his forehead shining with sweat, glowers at Grady.

Grady's face darkens, but he straightens his shoulders and doesn't budge.

I hear footsteps. Madison comes rushing up to us. She takes in the scene—Molly silently crying, Grady looking ready to punch the man, who looks ready to punch him back—and asks in a cool voice, "What's going on?"

"I'll tell you what the—" more language "—is going on." The man's face twists into a snarl, "these—" another stream of language words "—dogs attacked me and my dog. And one of them bit me. And probably bit Bubba here, too. I haven't had time to check him over. But I'll tell you what—" He gives Madison a triumphant look "—by the time my attorney is done, I'll own your house."

Madison sucks in her breath but otherwise doesn't react.

The man pulls out his phone and holds it up. "Gimme your name," he commands Molly.

Molly, her face wet with tears, stammers, "Mo—" but Madison interrupts.

"Sweetheart," she says, bending down to Molly. "I don't think this *stranger* needs your name, do you? I wonder if you happen to have your camera handy? We need to make sure that we have *all* the facts, and a few photos will help." Molly frowns, and then she nods in understanding, her hand already digging into her pocket.

Madison glances at Grady, giving him a nod. He instantly turns and hurries toward the house, Snippet at his side.

The man's eyes narrow in suspicion, but before he can say anything, Madison bats her eyes at him and asks in an innocent voice, "Could I ask, just for the record, what y'all are doing here in our yard?" She gives a meaningful look at the pile of poop a little distance away, then glances at Molly, who points her camera at him.

"It's not fenced," the man says belligerently. "And your dogs were loose. Dogs are not allowed off leash in unfenced yards, especially vicious dogs." He leans towards Molly. "Did you get that?"

Madison, still smiling, though her eyes are cold, says, "I'm sure she did. Could I have your name, please? Since you appear to be trespassing on our property?

"And if it's unfenced," Madison continues in a calm voice, "does that mean you think you have the right to use it for your dog's elimination? If you could give us your address, perhaps we could return the favor. We could trade yards, so to speak, you use ours for your dog and we'll use yours for ours. That way, neither of us has extra poop to scoop." She gives him a bright smile, tilting her head a bit in the way she often does when talking to men.

Grady comes back without Snippet, holding Madison's video camera, and lifts the camera up to his face, as the man keeps talking.

"Mel Blevins," he says. "But you don't need to write it down because my attorneys will be contacting you. In fact—" he taps the screen of his phone and says, "Okay, Google," a mysterious statement that people are using a lot these days. He pauses for a second then says, "Animal Control, Arlington, Virginia."

Molly gasps again, and Grady, with a little choking sound moves toward the man.

"Grady, honey," Madison says, in a low but steely voice, "stay focused." She glances in his direction. "Literally."

Grady raises the camera back to his face.

A faint voice comes from the man's phone. "Here is the number for Arlington Animal Control." He holds a finger above the screen, poised dramatically. "Got it."

"Hang on a second," Madison says, hurriedly.

The man's eyes are gloating. "Yeah?"

In a sweet tone, Madison says, "May we please see this alleged bite? For the record?" Her voice turns hard. "Because if you won't show it to us here, right now, I don't think you'll have a snowball's chance in—" she glances at Molly and Grady "—in a *very* hot place of winning a lawsuit against us."

He starts to speak, but she interrupts.

"And, *Mr.* Blevins, you ought to know that I happen to have a lawyer or two of my own. Since you've been so kind as to give me your name, let me give you mine. Madison Greene. Maybe you've heard of me? I blog for the *Low Down News*. I know lots of lawyers, good ones, who might even take this case pro bono for all the publicity I'm going to give it."

The man stares at her, open-mouthed, the smugness melting away. "You're that blog lady?"

"Yep. So, may we see this alleged bite?" Madison repeats. "Because I'm sure all my faithful watchers will want to see just how *very* badly you've been injured."

The man rubs a spot on the back of his hairy hand, but then rallies, squaring his shoulders. "You can't scare me, you—" and here he lets out a whole stream of "language" words. With a vicious yank on his poor dog's prong collar, he strides away.

No one speaks until the man turns into a yard near the far end of the block.

Then, Madison sighs. "Well, nothing like a cozy down-home welcome to our neighborhood. What a hateful creature. And I'm not talking about the dog."

But Molly, bending over me, isn't listening. "Doodle's ear's bleeding! That dog bit him." She holds out her hand, showing a couple of smears of blood on her fingers.

"How badly?" Madison asks. She and Molly lean over me, pulling on my ear.

"It's not deep," Madison says. "He just nicked the edge of his ear. But we could put some peroxide on it, just to be safe."

Molly nods. "That'd be great." Her voice is still shaky, as if she might cry. Not sure why. I don't feel the cut at all.

We go inside, and Molly and Madison take me into a small bathroom, which is a little crowded with the three of us. Grady, looking in, says, "I'm going out to the backyard with Snippet."

Madison drips some stuff on my ear that fizzes and burns a little. I'm relieved when she straightens up and says, "That ought to do it."

"Thanks." Molly twists a strand of hair, regarding Madison with anxious eyes. "Do we . . . I mean . . . do you . . ."

Madison says impatiently, "Spit it out, girl. What?"

"Do we have to tell my dad about what happened? I mean with the dogs? He might not let me bring Doodle again if he knew he got in a fight. Virginia has that one-bite law, and, even though he was protecting me, Doodle already has one bite."

"One bite law?" Madison asks, interested.

"Yeah. If a dog isn't like breaking the law by running loose or anything, and he bites someone, then the animal control people can't take him away. Because any dog could bite someone in the right situation. But if a dog bites more than once, then he might be declared a vicious dog and could get . . ." her voice cracks . . . "put down."

"Mr. Doodle here bit someone?" Madison asks in amazement. "Who'd he bite?"

I'm trying to remember myself, memory never being one of my strengths. Live for the now is my motto, which I might have mentioned before.

"This guy at a cert trial who was trying to hurt me. He's in jail now for fraud."

Now it's coming back to me. That was quite a day. Much more exciting than cert trials usually are, that's for sure.

"And then there was that burglar, but he was pointing a gun on me, so that doesn't count." Molly, twisting her hair furiously, continues, "And since the other guy *is* in jail and Doodle had a good reason, it might not count either. But what if it does?"

Madison rests a hand on Molly's shoulder. "Honey, I don't think you have to worry. First, that foul-mouthed neighbor of ours has absolutely no proof that either Doodle or Snippet bit him, you understand? He wouldn't show us the bite, remember? And, second, any judge would say that a bite to save a child doesn't mean a dog is vicious."

"Dad says it doesn't matter what a judge would say because we couldn't afford the court costs if we had to prove Doodle innocent." Molly's eyes well with tears.

Madison says, "Honey, you're really worrying about this, aren't you?" Molly nods without speaking.

Madison gives her a quick hug. "Well, stop worrying because that man will never know your name, so whatever he does will not affect you."

More nodding. Molly yanks a couple of tissues from a box on the toilet and wipes her eyes. "But do we have to tell Dad?"

"Tell him what?" Madison gives Molly a conspiratorial smile. "That a crazy neighbor made up a silly story because he was caught using our lawn as his dog's favorite potty spot? I wouldn't want to burden the man with such nonsense."

Molly sighs with relief, and grins back at her.

"But that one-bite law—now I'm going to put that knowledge to some good use. I'll bet Mr. Blevins doesn't know about that. Bet he's a transplant from another state."

Molly gives her another grin, then says, "Thanks."

Much happier, Molly takes me out to join Grady and Snippet in the backyard, where we practice for the Canine Good Citizen test. This means Snippet and I have to do a few easy things like stand still when someone pets us, and not bark when we meet strange people or dogs, and stay quietly on a leash while our handler walks some distance away. Couldn't be simpler, especially, as I've said before, compared to the scent-detection tests I have to take for my bed-bug job.

When the boss shows up to take us home, Madison insists on giving him a tour of the house first.

"Sure," the boss says, rubbing his beard, which means he's not sure at all. Since the video-blog incident, the boss always acts uncomfortable around Madison and often tries to avoid her, even though he's no longer angry at her.

Madison never looks like she wants to avoid the boss. She's always tilting her head, pushing back her long curls, and giving him wide-eyed smiles. She does this now, as she leads the boss through the house.

And then it's time for us to go home. Molly loads me into my wire crate, which is bolted to the floor of the van behind the front seats, and, with a wave to Grady, climbs into the front seat.

"Great house," the boss says, backing the van out of the driveway. "Double garage." His voice is filled with envy. "Bet she paid a pretty penny."

"I don't know how much," Molly says, "but Grady told me she kept threatening to look at homes in other cities because Arlington is so pricy. She said they could have had a newer, bigger home somewhere else."

"I believe it. So why didn't she do that?"

"Grady doesn't want to change schools, and she didn't want a long drive."

"That makes sense. But it'd sure be tempting." The boss starts to tap his fingers on the steering wheel.

Molly turns her head to look at him and I can hear the alarm in her voice. "But we wouldn't move, would we?"

"Not in my plans," the boss says cheerfully. "Not unless something happened and we had to." He taps some more, then says, "So, how'd it go? Did you and Grady get a good practice in?"

Molly only hesitates a fraction of a second before she answers. "Yeah. Great. Everything went really great."

Chapter 3

Dog Days

ANYONE COULD SMELL THAT MOLLY AND GRADY ARE anxious. I mean any of the many dogs milling about here in the park, of course, or the ones ahead of us in line. The humans holding their leashes couldn't smell their way out of a paper bag, if you catch my drift. But to the dogs, their anxiety would be obvious.

The boss, on the other hand, isn't as much anxious as impatient. He glances at his phone and then at the table, where a round-bodied woman wearing a baseball hat and a bright windbreaker sits studying a stack of papers.

"Twenty-three minutes late," he says glumly, rubbing his beard. Both he and Molly are wearing their Hunter Bed-Bug Detection parkas, but open, not zipped. "I think it'd be more worthwhile if they changed the competition from Canine Good Citizen to Human Good Organization and see how those bozos fared."

Molly grins and says, "Right, Dad."

Grady runs a hand through his straight-up hair. Then he wipes both hands on his jeans, which, now that I notice, don't have holes in the knees like the ones he usually wears. And there are no pictures of zombies on his T-shirt, at least none I can see in the part showing under his windbreaker.

Come to think of it, Molly changed outfits twice before we left home, and now she's twisting a strand of hair, a sure sign she's nervous. Not that I didn't already know that, with the sharp scent of tension pouring from her.

Molly says, "Don't worry. Snippet will do great. She really wants to please you."

As if to prove my point, Snippet licks Grady's fingers. He runs a hand lightly down her silky red coat, which Madison likes to say will probably soon be shed all over her furniture.

We're standing in line in front of a table that sits under the shade of a giant pine tree. The scents of dirt and pine needles, and, of course, dog pee, rise from the trunk and the pale new grass around it. A sweeter (though less interesting) odor wafts from the flowers covering several nearby trees. On the other side of the table is a small field enclosed with one of those wobbly portable fences you always see at dog shows.

We're waiting our turn to be tested, which is taking a long time because, according to the boss, the judges have "the organizational skills of a gnat." No idea what he means, because I haven't seen any gnats today at all. They can be tasty if you snap up a mouthful. But the breeze on my coat feels too cool to have gnats.

So far, we've only seen one dog go into the field, a black and tan hound, whose elderly handler walks as if his knees have trouble bending.

"I think I'll sit down," the boss says, gesturing at a line of folding chairs along the outside of the fence-off area and heading toward them.

Just as the boss is taking a seat, a voice, high and loud calls out, "Grady!" It comes from a girl almost as tall as Grady, but much thinner. She's walking alongside a stockier, dark-haired woman and a boy, but now she pulls ahead, hurrying confidently toward us, chin up.

Less confident is the young chocolate Lab trotting beside her, his tail low. "Chocolate" means the dog's coat color, of course, and has nothing to do with the candy, something I didn't always know and found confusing for a while, especially since chocolate is supposed to be bad for dogs. Trust me, there's no hint of the candy in the scent of this dog.

"Hi, Hailey." Grady doesn't seem especially happy to see her. Hailey has dark hair that reaches halfway to her waist, pale skin, and wide brown eyes darkened with eyeliner, which—just a note here—isn't good to eat. However, the shiny, pointy-toed boots she's wearing, that come halfway up her tight jeans, give off a tempting leathery smell and would be fun to chew on if shoes, like chocolate, weren't forbidden to dogs.

Hailey looks down at the Lab and commands, "Hershey, sit." Hershey, stretched out to sniff noses with me and Snippet, eases back and sits at her side. He seems polite enough for a pup and comfortable with other dogs.

"Hershey?" Grady asks, scratching behind the dog's ears.

"Yeah. His official AKC name is Hailey's Hershey Chocolate Kiss." Hailey bends down to pet Hershey, who wags his tail but shrinks ever so slightly from her touch. Hailey, smiling, doesn't seem to notice.

Her companions stop a little ways from us. The woman kind of looks like a heavier version of Molly's mother, with her brown skin, dark hair pulled back into a bun (not the kind you eat), and black eyes. The boy beside her is almost as tall as Molly, but thinner and younger. He's wearing jeans and a hooded sweatshirt, and bright athletic shoes that are higher in the front than at the heel and have multicolored laces. The woman pulls a phone up to her ear and begins to talk in Spanish.

At the sound of her voice, Molly and Grady glance curiously in her direction.

"That's Dominga, my nanny," Hailey says, following their gaze. She beams at the woman fondly, then frowns slightly. "She's having babysitting problems—kind of funny for a nanny, right?—because her aunt usually watches Mario—" she tilts her head towards the boy—"and this aunt had a stroke and is in the hospital. I told my mom I'd be okay here by myself and she should let Dominga have the day off, because, it's Saturday, and I'm not like six, right? And I have Hershey to protect me. But my mom thinks because of my dad's job—kind of secret but *really* important, you know?—that I can't be left alone. Ever. She says I could be kidnapped. So Dominga had to bring Mario along, which she hardly ever does."

Hershey, his tail low, looks more the type to run rather than protect.

Hailey sighs, then turns to Grady. "So, you're doing this, too? Didn't know you had a dog." She pats Snippet on the head. "Beautiful dog. What kind is he?"

"She's an Irish golden," Grady says. "Irish setter, golden retriever mix. At least, that's what we think. With maybe a touch of Border collie, because she's smaller than most Irish goldens. I just got her a few months ago."

"Oh. A designer dog." Hailey gives him a pitying look.

Grady frowns. "Probably more accidental than designed. We don't know where she came from."

"Hershey's only seven months old, but he's been doing so well that my trainer—Ned Gurly of Champion Labs?—"

When both Molly and Grady give her blank looks, Hailey flips a few strands of hair from her face and says a little defensively, "he's *nationally* famous. Anyway, he suggested I try him out for the Canine Good Citizen test." She gives Hershey a pat on the head. "Because he can be shy in crowds. He thought it'd be good experience, because he's so motivated."

I can be motivated if the treats are good. Just sayin'.

When Grady and Molly still remain silent, Hailey asks, "Who do you train with?"

Grady's frown deepens. He shifts his weight from one foot to another.

Molly, her voice a little strained, says, "We're doing it ourselves."

"Molly's studying to be a dog trainer," Grady adds. "She works with—"

"Molly?" Hailey gapes as if seeing Molly for the first time. She frowns. "Do I know you?"

An odd question, in my opinion, since I'd think Hailey would know who she knows, if you get what I mean. Hershey rises and goes back to sniffing noses with Snippet.

"She's in the other fifth grade class—Ms. Mandisa's," Grady says. "Not ours."

Hailey is in Grady's class? She looks much younger, even with the black eyeliner. However, Grady is a big guy, partly (according to the boss) because his dad had him start school a year late in hopes that he would play football, something the boss finds amusing. "He's got the weight but not the muscle," the boss likes to say. Which works out for Grady, who has said more than once that he hates sports. Until he got Snippet, Grady's favorite thing was wearing zombie T-shirts and playing video games.

Hailey smiles at Molly and leans over to pat me on the head, something I'm not fond of. "Is that a standard poodle?"

"Labradoodle," Molly says. "He's a bed-bug dog."

"Oh. Looks like a poodle."

I get that a lot, mostly because of my curly hair. And, as I mentioned before, because I'm more like a poodle in personality. "Much more doodle than labra," was how one trainer put it, not meaning it as a compliment for reasons I can't imagine.

Hailey gives me another pat and I try not to shrink away from her touch. "We thought about getting a labradoodle—the whole non-shedding thing, right?—but Ned says designer dogs have problems and it's always better to go purebred, so we should pick a poodle or a Labrador."

Molly says stiffly, "Doodle's a certified bed-bug dog. He can—"

"Oh, I'm sure he's fine," Hailey says with a twist of her fingers. "It's just I guess Ned said labradoodles can have . . . issues."

The only issue I have at the moment is that Hailey seems to be making both Molly and Grady angry.

Molly, her jaw tightly set, stares at the ground.

"No issues with Doodle," Grady says, his face flushing.

Hailey doesn't seem to have heard. "Anyway, when I saw Hershey—he was such a cute puppy with giant paws, and both his parents are *national* champions—that decided it."

Neither Molly nor Grady say anything. After a bit, Hailey asks Grady "So, is this the only thing you're entered in?"

"Yeah, for now." Grady answers. "I'm thinking about training her for disc dogs or agility."

"We're doing the Good Citizen—obviously," Hailey says, smiling down at Hershey, "and the AKC puppy conformation, which—" She gives Grady a sympathetic look—"I guess you couldn't enter."

"Yeah," Grady agrees. "Snippet's almost three."

"No. I meant because your dog isn't a purebred." Her lips stretch into a smug line. "But it's good that they have some things for mixed breeds, like disc catching and such. So they're not left out, you know?"

Grady gives her a sour look and I hear Molly exhale.

"What's your time slot?"

"Two-twenty," Grady says tersely. "Molly's at two-thirty."

"Oh, I'm just before you, then," Hailey says. "Two-ten."

She pulls her phone out of her pocket. "Ack. Already five after. Good luck!" She runs over to Dominga, still on the phone, gives her a quick hug, and then marches up to the front of the line.

"Hailey Kensington," she says in loud voice, to the cheerful-looking woman with the big hat.

The woman smiles and soon Hailey and Hershey walk onto the field.

"Good luck," Grady says in a low voice, mimicking Hailey's tone.

"My trainer's nationally famous." Molly rolls her eyes. "Bet he couldn't train bed-bug dogs. Bet he's no better than Miguel."

Have to agree. I've never met anyone better with dogs than Miguel, not even the service-dog trainers I had when I was a pup.

"She has a chauffeur drive her to school," Grady says. "Her dad's some bigwig in the state department, can't remember what, and Mama says her mother is richer than rich."

They both watch Hailey and Hershey walk out into the field.

Hershey keeps his head right by Hailey's knee and his eyes fixed on Hailey's closed hand. Just before they get to the first station, Hailey touches her hand against Hershey's nose.

"Did you see that?" Molly asks in a low voice.

"What?" Grady asks.

"I think she slipped Hershey a treat."

She did indeed. Saw it myself. There's no missing something like that. According to Molly, a handler can't give a dog treats during the test. A silly rule, obviously designed by humans.

Grady frowns. "Let's hope one of the judges saw it."

Molly grabs her camera from the pocket of her windbreaker and points it at Hailey. She holds it steady as Hailey shakes the hand of a man standing under a beach umbrella, and then moves towards the next station. "Got it!" Molly says with some satisfaction.

Not sure what she means, but then cameras have always been a bit of a mystery for me. Not the objects themselves, but how Molly can point it one way or another and click it—what she calls "taking pictures"—which, it turns out, somehow become pictures on her computer.

According to her, it all depends upon these little things she calls her memory cards. Sometimes she calls them the brains of her camera. They certainly don't look or smell like any brains I've ever seen, which have been mostly of the rabbit variety. Frankly, they'd be much more interesting if they did. But rather, they're small pieces of plastic that mostly smell like Molly's hands and, well, plastic.

One time she lost a memory card, and was really worried it was lost forever, which was bad because it had some important pictures, but in a stroke of pure luck, I managed to find it for her while I was kind of looking for something else. Since then, she's trained me to search for the memory cards in the same way that I do bed bugs. The boss calls this "locking the stable door after the horse has been stolen," a truly baffling statement, as there's never been a horse anywhere near us when I'm doing the searching. But the point is, now that I understand what to sniff out, I can find the card without being lucky.

Grady shifts his weight and glances at his phone. "I guess we're up." He takes Snippet to the hat woman behind the table, who flashes him a big smile. She's dressed one of those flowery patterned blouses like nurses sometimes wear. "Grady Greene?" she asks.

Molly waves to the boss, then holds her camera toward Grady, staring at the screen as Grady and Snippet walk across the grass to the man under the umbrella. Snippet keeps her eyes on Grady and doesn't pull. Grady keeps his fingers open and doesn't slip her any treats.

"Good job," Molly says softly, her camera still on Grady.

"Next," says the lady at the table.

"That's us." Molly shoves the camera into the pocket of her windbreaker. At the table, Molly hands the smiling lady a piece of paper. "Molly Hunter and Doodle," she says. And then it's our turn to walk onto the field.

We stop when the first man comes over and shakes Molly's hand. I sit quietly. Like I said, easy, right? Except I catch the distinct sour scent of tension. I lift my nose. Not coming from the man, whose prevailing scent is cigarette smoke, but on the breeze, which is blowing from the direction of where the boss is sitting. I work my nostrils, sampling the air. Not from Grady. He's walking away from us, downwind. Not the boss.

Maybe the teenage guy standing next to the fence just beyond the folding chairs? I stare at him. Something furtive in his body language makes the hair rise on my back. He has a baseball cap on, pulled low. He's staring at something. I follow his gaze across the field to a girl, also wearing a baseball cap, who stands on the opposite side of the fence. And then, the guy moves his hand in a way that reminds me of a handler signaling a command to a dog. The girl nods and holds up her thumb. No idea what's going on, but my instincts tell me it's nothing good. I growl softly.

"Hush," Molly whispers, alarmed. "Come on." I hurry to catch up, keeping my eye on first the guy and then the girl. Suddenly, the guy's arm thrusts forward and something comes hurtling towards us.

I bark.

"Doo—!" Molly's voice is cut off by several loud pops, and a sudden explosion of brightly colored smoke, and, after that, the piercing sound of Hailey's voice.

Chapter 4

Another Surprise

HERSHEY! *HERSHEY!*" HAILEY SCREAMS.
I glance back at the teen on the fence and bark again, but he has already turned and is walking rapidly away. I keep my eyes on him, barking.

Molly grabs her camera from her pocket and clicks it at the cloud of colored smoke just ahead of us, but then says to me, "What is it?" She turns toward the guy, his back now to us and his hat off. Her camera clicks a few times before he disappears into the crowd of people rushing toward us.

Hailey's still screaming. "Hershey! Hershey!"

And then, Hershey dashes towards us, running along the fence, his leash flying behind him. Hershey's face and back are no longer the color of chocolate but brightly colored like the smoke. He's clearly panicked, his tail between his legs, ears flattened, and his eyes rimmed with white.

Molly shouts his name, but he races by with no sign that he heard. She dives for his leash, but misses it. For a moment, it looks like he might try to go right through the wobbly fence, but he veers and runs alongside it.

And then, people began pouring onto the field.

"Molly! Are you okay?" The boss rushes up to her, studies her a second and then pulls her into a hug. He takes her hand. "Let's get out of—"

"Molly!" Grady emerges from the other side of the smoke. Like Hershey, he and Snippet are also covered in the bright dust. Unlike Hershey, though, Snippet isn't panicked. She trots alongside Grady, watching all the people with interest.

"You okay?" the boss and Molly ask at the same time.

"Yeah. Just—some kind of paint bombs, I think."

"Anyone hurt?" the boss asks.

"Everyone's fine." Grady wipes his forehead and stares at the dust on his fingers "Just filthy."

"What about Hailey?" Molly looks over to where the smoke has now formed a cloud rising and stretching into the breeze. Hailey, now surrounded by a cluster of people, has at last stopped screaming.

Dominga passes us, hurrying onto the field, Mario behind her. Soon, Hailey is sobbing in her arms while Mario stands a little ways away, looking distinctly unhappy.

"She's okay. One of those smoke bombs landed practically on top of her. Sure spooked Hershey." Grady stares across the field. "Oh. Good. Looks like someone finally caught him."

Molly clicks more photos. Grady watches her a second and pulls out his phone. "Better let Mama know about this," he says. "She'd kill me if she missed the story."

Grady stares at his phone, then his mouth tightens briefly. "Must still be in her interview." He pauses a second. "Hey, Mama," he says in that tone people use when there's no voice at the other end. "Someone threw a couple of paint bombs into the arena here at the park. I'm fine. No one was hurt, but it's kind of chaotic here. Might be a good story."

The loudspeaker spits and crackles, and then a voice says, "Attention! Everyone please stay where you are. We have officers coming to assist you. I repeat: Please stay where you are. Officers are coming to assist you."

At this, on the other side of the fence, a middle-aged woman with frizzy curls down to her waist, glances around in alarm and hurries away. Several other people do as well.

"Looks like some people don't want to be questioned," Grady says, watching.

Molly clicks her camera at their backs. Then she turns to Grady. "Smile." She snaps a bunch more photos.

Grady runs a hand down Snippet's back and then wipes it on his pants. "I hope this stuff isn't toxic. It's all over both of us."

"I saw a roll of paper towels at the desk," Molly says.

"Good idea." Grady hands Snippet's leash to Molly, and runs back to the entrance, returning shortly with a huge wad of paper towels.

Meanwhile, a thick man in a uniform who walks like his shoes pinch his toes, strides onto the field. "I'm with security," he says in a loud voice. "Everyone stay put. The police are on their way and will need your statements."

So, we all stand around while colorful clouds wisp up into the sky and disappear. Grady tries to call his mother again and leaves another message.

Finally I hear the unmistakable wail of sirens.

"There's the police," Molly says a few moments later.

Before long, cars with flashing lights speed into the parking lots. Car doors slam and boots thud as the police hurry toward us.

And then a slender, dark-haired woman, not in uniform, approaches us. Hey, I recognize her!

Molly does, too. She stiffens, her eyes wide. "Mom?"

"Molly!" Cori sounds as surprised as Molly looks. She gives the boss a curt nod. "Hey, Josh. What are you guys doing here?"

Cori's gaze is on the boss, but Molly is the one who answers. "Doodle's Canine Good Citizen test, remember? I told you we'd be doing it today. You said you had to work." Molly's hand steals up to twist a strand of hair.

"Oh. That's right. And if I hadn't had to work already, I'd be called in now." She waves a hand at the cluster of people on the field.

Cori often has to work when Molly invites her to things, partly because she's a cop. The first time we discovered that—a long story that involved gunfire—she was undercover, which I learned has nothing to do with blankets but meant she was pretending to be someone else. Turns out her real name is Cori Vega. She left Molly and the boss when Molly was young, something that sometimes makes Molly sad and the boss angry, although not as much as it used to. But Molly still tends to get nervous whenever she's around her mother, which is why it doesn't surprise me that she's twisting her hair.

Cori has a big badge pinned on her blouse, so I don't think she's undercover today.

"We've got practically the whole department here," she says with a grimace. "Thought it was a terrorist attack at first." She sighs. "Or a kidnapping attempt. Looks like we over-reacted, but these days we never know." She gives Molly a quick hug, then looks her over. "Are you okay?"

"We're fine. Grady thinks it was just some kind of paint bomb."

Cori nods. "Yeah, that's what we think now. Look, I got to get to work. Has anyone taken your statements yet?"

Grady and Molly shake their heads.

"Well, wait here, then."

"Okay if we go over to the chairs?" the boss asks.

Cori says, "Sure," her eyes already on a group of cops talking to Hailey, who wails, "Kidnap me," in a loud voice. Someone must have brought Hershey back, because Mario, standing a little ways away, is holding his leash and stroking him under his chin.

Cori heads toward them while we walk back through the gate to the chairs alongside the fence. Snippet plops down on the ground, panting, and Grady squats beside her.

Everybody seems busy. Everyone but us, that is. The cops move from person to person, talking and taking notes. Meanwhile, we sit and watch, which, frankly, soon becomes boring. A tall blonde woman, wearing knee-length boots much like Hailey's, walks briskly past us and rushes over to pull Hailey into a long hug. After that, she talks briefly with Dominga. Mario hands Hershey's leash to Hailey, and he and his mother leave.

Molly keeps snapping photos and at one point Grady says, "Good idea," and starts taking pictures with his phone.

Finally Cori comes back to us. "Sorry that took so long," she says. "Thanks for waiting. I'll just get Grady's statement here—" she glances at Molly "—and yours and Josh's after that." Notebook in hand, she turns to Grady. "So, tell me what you saw."

Grady clears his throat—he does this a lot when he's nervous—and leans forward. "I'd just finished the third section of the Canine Good Citizen test, the one to see if a dog will accept a groomer." He adds, in explanation, "A stranger has to handle the dog's paws and run a brush over the dog's back." He shifts his weight again. "And then, we were going toward this group, a man and two women, for the part on walking through a crowd." Again, in explanation, "The dog has to walk past the people without reacting. But we hadn't gotten to the group yet. Hailey was ahead of us, at the next station. And then there was this 'pop, pop, pop' and smoke everywhere and Hailey was screaming."

His eyes widen a little as he says this. "I thought . . . at first, I thought she might have been shot. Or hit by a real bomb. 'Cause one of the paint bombs exploded right beside her. One was a little ways from Snippet and me." He pauses, swallowing hard. Snippet whines softly and licks his hand. "Hailey thought someone was trying to kidnap her. She kept screaming."

Cori says. "Did you see anything at all before it hit? Anyone who might have thrown it?"

Grady shakes his head. "I was looking ahead at the group," he says. "Didn't see or hear anything until it hit."

Molly straightens up. "Doodle saw something, I think. He barked just before it hit. At something over on—" she hesitates for a second "—on the left side of where we were." She points to the section of fence on the other side of the chairs. "I started to correct him because he can't pass the test if he barks. But now I think he barked because he saw something."

Of course I saw something. Like I would bark at nothing! At least not usually. The teenager with the baseball cap and the scent of tension. I remember it.

"Okay," Cori says, scribbling on her pad. "Anything else? Either of you?"

"Well . . ." Molly pauses again. Her hand slips to her pocket, the one with the camera, and she hesitates, but then says, "Nothing. I wasn't looking at the crowd."

"Okay, great. Josh?"

"Had my eyes glued to Grady and then Molly the whole time," the boss says. "I saw Doodle turn in my direction and bark, but I just thought—well, you know Doodle. I was worried he wouldn't pass."

Seriously?

Cori nods. "I guess that's it then. I'd better get back . . ." she looks uncertainly at Molly, then gives her a quick hug before walking back to the field.

Molly, frowning a little, watches her go.

The loudspeaker makes a grating sound and the same man's voice we heard earlier says, "Hey folks. Well, that put a crimp in our shorts, didn't it?" He gives a little chuckle. "I'm happy to report that no one was hurt in this little incident. It appears that several paint bombs were tossed into the obedience arena. We don't know who is responsible yet. The police and park security personnel are conducting a thorough investigation and will be here in force for tomorrow's events. That's right, folks. We will go ahead with our regularly planned schedule of events tomorrow. But we're going to close down early today to help these good folks figure out what happened. Be sure to check your phones and emails for updates on rescheduled events. And, for all of you involved in the Canine Good Citizen test, we will be rescheduling it for tomorrow, starting at ten o'clock. That's starting tomorrow, at ten, for the Canine Good Citizen test.

Be sure to ask at the desk for your individual time. The rest of tomorrow's events will go on as scheduled. We appreciate your patience and support."

The boss says, "That's optimistic. No patience or support from me."

And with that, we all turn and head for the parking lot.

Chapter 5

HEAR

WHEN WE GET TO THE VAN, THE BOSS OPENS ALL
the doors and lifts the back hatch. In spite of the chilly
breeze, the air coming from the van is hot. "Cool it off a bit," he
says.

Grady tells the boss he can drop him off at his house, but the
boss shakes his head. "How 'bout you come home with us until
your mom is done. I don't like you home alone."

Grady shrugs. "Do it all the time."

"Well, it's not necessary today," the boss says firmly. "I can
run you home after she gets back." He gives Grady and Snippet
a long look. "Just a second." He reaches into the very back and
grabs several of the towels he uses to dry my paws when it rains.
He spreads them over the backseat.

"For you," he says to Grady with a grin. "We don't need a paint
job on the seats. Even if it is water soluble. Snippet can go in the
very back—I already have a layer of sheets down."

The boss calls to Snippet, who jumps up into the van, while
Grady, still clutching a wad of paper towels, edges around my
crate onto the back seat. Then Molly puts me in my crate, a wire

cage in the center of the van. It's bolted to the floor so that, as the boss likes to say, "If there's an accident, my prime business asset doesn't go sailing through the window."

Molly takes her usual position up front by the boss.

"Hot," Grady says, wiping his forehead and then staring at the stains on the paper towel. I have to agree. I'm panting. But pretty soon, as always, the air shooting from the vents in the car turns cold.

When it's finally cool enough for the boss to turn down the fan so it doesn't make such a racket, Molly turns in her seat to face Grady. "Do you think someone was trying to kidnap Hailey?"

"There wasn't anyone there trying to grab her," Grady answers. Then, straightening up in his chair, "I bet I know who did it. HEAR."

"Here?" Molly looks confused.

"H.E.A.R.," Grady says, spelling out each letter. "It stands for Humanitarians for Enlightened Animal Relations. Mama did a big piece on them a few weeks ago. They don't believe anyone should have pets at all, that we should respect—" he squints, thinking "—the individual sovereignty of animals. They consider pet ownership to be slavery."

The boss snorts, his eyes on the road. "As if feral dogs and cats lead a better life than our pampered pets!"

Pampered? Hardly. I do my job and get paid, just like the boss.

"Yeah," Grady agrees. "That's what Mama said in her piece. Wild dogs have heartworm and fleas and all sorts of diseases."

"Rabies," Molly adds. "Not to mention they often are half-starved."

"But it's not just that," Grady says. "HEAR runs all sorts of ads—these heartbreaking ones showing some malnourished dog in a cage—and talk about how they rescue dogs and cats so people will donate, but it turns out they kill almost all the animal they supposedly rescue."

Molly's eyes turn dark with alarm. "They don't run no-kill shelters?"

"More like 'all-kill' shelters. Over 99 percent. At least, that's what Mama said in her blog. And now, this one family says HEAR people stole their dog from their porch—they caught it on their security camera—and when they went the next day to get the dog, they were told it had already been euthanized."

"How can they get away with that?" the boss asks. "Stealing pets? Someone would sue their pants off."

"Yeah, you'd think. But Mama says they target poor neighborhoods where the people can't afford to hire lawyers. She was pretty upset about it, and her blog got like a zillion comments and some people started a big fund-raiser for the family to sue HEAR."

"I bet that made her unpopular," the boss says. "With the HEAR people, I mean."

"Yeah," Grady says. "You think they were trying to hit me with the paint bomb? Because of Mama's blog?"

No one speaks for a moment. "Just as likely to be aimed at the whole pet show as you, I'd think," the boss says. "And we don't know who did it. Might not be HEAR at all."

Before long, we're home. Molly and Grady take me and Snippet to the backyard to pee. I let Snippet pee first, then make sure to go on top of hers.

Grady calls his mother again and this time gets her. She promises to swing by and pick him up on her way home, which she says won't be long.

Molly and Grady go inside, but Snippet and I have to stay in the yard because of the paint on her. Not that we mind. Outside is where we can play. We're in the middle of a great chasing game, when a car honks from the driveway, and then Grady gets Snippet and hurries out the door.

Later, after dinner, the boss watches basketball on TV while Molly looks at her photos on her computer. I stay with Molly because—trust me—basketball is pretty boring, although not as bad as football, the most boring game on earth. Not that Molly staring at her computer screen is much more interesting, but at least it's not noisy with people yammering on endlessly. Sometimes, she plays music, but tonight she just flips through screen after screen of photos.

"Don't see anything," she says at one point. And a little later. "Except, maybe . . ."

She leans forward and studies the screen. I can tell that it's a photo of the park where we were earlier. There's a man standing a ways behind the fence. No scent, of course, so he could be anyone.

Molly's phone bursts into a short tune, the same as one of her favorite songs.

"Hey, Grady," she says. "Did the paint come off?"

Grady's voice comes through the phone. "Oh. Yeah. I bathed Snippet then had to wash out the tub, but it's all gone now. Mama was bummed that she missed out on everything, since she's already done stories on HEAR. Hey," his voice suddenly sounds strained. "She wants to talk to you for a second. That okay?"

"Yeah." Molly sounds puzzled. Through the phone—have I mentioned my hearing is excellent, much better than any human's?—I hear Grady say, "*You* ask her. I'm not going to."

And then, Madison's voice comes through.

"Hey, honey," she says, "I didn't realize there was so much drama at the park today. I should have asked you this when I came to get Grady. He says you took photos after the paint bomb today? Any chance you'd let me take a peek? If I use one, I'll pay you the same as last time."

Molly hesitates for a second. "Okay, I guess."

"I'm sorry I missed all the excitement. I can't believe how Grady looked! I was stuck in this interview with some attorneys and—" she sighs. "Let's just say with all the imagination that went into what they were claiming, I felt hip-high in cow dung which no means of escape. Paint would have been less stinky, if you get what I'm saying."

No clue here, and Molly seems a bit confused herself.

"And they went on foooor-ever. I grew old in that interview."

Molly smiles briefly at this.

"And the head honcho, a slimy son-of—" she stops—"I mean the kind of man you think was spawned under a rock—had the nerve to threaten me. 'Better be careful what you air,' he said. 'Unless you're up for a lot of trouble.'" She sighs. "Well, I got lawyers, too, although I don't have an unlimited budget like they seem to. Anyway, that's why I wasn't there to see Grady today. But I'd really be grateful to you forever if I could see those photos tonight."

Molly blinks, then glances at her computer. "If you bring me a flash drive, I could copy the photos for you. I just looked through them and didn't see anything really suspicious." Molly pauses for a second. "I'll need to give a copy to my mom if she wants them."

"That's fine. I'm mostly after a good shot or two after the paint bombs hit," Madison says. "Grady says he was covered from head to toe."

Another smile. "Yeah. I could give Grady a copy tomorrow. We have to repeat the CGC test in the morning."

"You could give it to *me* tomorrow," Madison says firmly, "because I'll be there. Wouldn't miss it for the world. Your daddy going to be there?"

"Yeah," Molly's brow suddenly creases. "And maybe Annie," she says with a trace of defiance.

"Well, it'll just be a reunion then. But here's the thing about the photos. I'd rather see them tonight. Old news is no news, as my daddy used to say. Could I possibly run by and have you copy them tonight? Only take a second."

"I guess. Hang on a sec."

Molly puts down her phone and goes into the living room to explain the situation to the boss.

"Okay with me, I guess."

When Molly gets back to the phone, Madison says, "Well, then I'll be seeing y'all in a few minutes. Bye now."

The boss clicks off the TV and moves to his bedroom. "So I don't have to entertain her," he says, closing the door.

But, a little while later, it's Grady who knocks, handing her a flash drive when Molly invites him in. "Sorry about this. Mama's crazy to see your photos. I gave her the ones on my phone, but those were taken later."

"It's okay," Molly says. "I'm saving money for a better camera, so it'll be great if she wants one."

Molly takes the little piece of plastic—don't know why they call it a drive since it has nothing to do with cars—and sticks it in her computer. I curl down on the rug while she and Grady talk about the events tomorrow. Heard it all before, so I drift off to sleep, and the next thing I know, Molly's saying goodbye to Grady and then calling me to go outside to pee before bedtime.

Chapter 6

Tanya

TODAY WE'RE GOING BACK TO THE PARK, AND—GOOD
news!—Molly's best friend Tanya gets to go with us. Molly
and Tanya are in the same class at school, but—can't remember if I've mentioned this—I first met Tanya and Mrs. Franklin
when I sort of got lost and ended up in front of their home.
We've been great friends ever since. Mrs. Franklin calls me her
"substitute dog."

Tanya's got the front door open and is hurrying towards us as
soon as we pull into the Franklin's driveway. Takes me a second
to recognize her, because she's wearing a baseball hat, which
I've never seen her do before.

Molly jumps out and joins Tanya on the back seat, behind
my crate.

"Mama made me wear this," Tanya says, pulling off the hat
and laying it on the seat. Her hair, black and curly like my own
except much longer, is pulled back into two braids. "She says
black skin can get sunburned as well as white, and the sun's
as strong in cool weather as it is in hot, so I have to keep my
face out of the sun so I don't end up with skin cancer when

I'm thirty." Tanya shakes her head at the idea, but the boss says, "Smart woman!"

Mrs. Franklin, Tanya's mom *is* smart, but even better, in my opinion, she's nice, always giving me extra treats when we're at her house.

"Speaking of which, did you bring sunscreen?" the boss asks Molly. "Supposed to be bright with temps in the fifties, which might break a record for the first week in March."

Molly says, "Yeah." She holds up her purse, the one with the shoulder strap that she sometimes uses to carry her phone and camera. "In here." She and Tanya share a look. The boss turns on the radio but keeps the volume low.

Soon the girls are talking a mile a minute—that's what the boss calls it when they get going—which means really fast. Molly tells Tanya all about Grady and Snippet getting hit by the paint bombs, and then how Grady thinks it's because of HEAR.

"Humanitarians for Enlightened Animal Relations," Molly says. "Grady says they stole a dog from this family's porch, and by the time they tried to get the dog, it'd already been euthanized."

Wait. I thought Grady said the dog had been killed. Is that what *euthanize* means? An alarming thought, especially since Miguel, my old trainer, has said more than once that he rescued me the day before I was supposed to be euthanized. Whoa. Don't want to think about that.

But Tanya's all excited "—heard Mama talking to the Carters. Remember Dan? The blind Jack Russell of theirs?"

Molly shakes her head.

"Mrs. Carter's a neighbor," Tanya says, explaining, "and her dog Dan—he's blind—*never* goes off their porch. It's all screened in so Dan can't get out. Not that he would, 'cause he's scared 'cause he can't see. But Mama said Mrs. Carter went grocery shopping the other day and left Dan on their porch 'cause the weather was nice, and when she came home, Dan was gone. And someone said there was this suspicious white van cruising the neighborhood. So Mama said Mrs. Carter thought someone might have stolen him, but who would steal a blind dog, even if it is a Jack Russell?" She looks at Molly, wide-eyed. "Do you think . . . ?"

"I don't know," Molly says. "That'd be awful. Poor Dan." She stares ahead, her eyes unfocused for a minute. "We could tell Madison—remember Grady's mom?"

Tanya tilts her head, pretends to smooth her hair back and then blinks at Molly in an oddly exaggerated way, "Y'all think I could forget? Thank yee-uu darlin.'"

Both girls giggle and the boss turns down the radio and glances in the mirror. "What's so funny?" he asks. To which they both call out, "Nothing!" and giggle some more. But then Molly says, in a serious tone, "She's actually really nice when you get to know her. She's been, um, helpful to me."

Tanya nods. "Buys your photos!"

"Yeah, and other stuff." Molly glances at the boss and says in a very quiet voice, "can't tell you now."

Before long, the van slows down. Hey, we're at the park.

"Everybody and their dog is here today," the boss mutters, as he drives from one parking lot to another looking for a space. Finally he finds one, much further away than where we were before. The boss makes the girls put on sunscreen on their face and hands—can't say I like the smell—and then on their arms in case it gets warm enough that they take off the hoodies they're both wearing. He slathers some on his face and neck as well, and Tanya puts on her hat. We walk across the asphalt, which has several nosefuls of interesting smells, but I don't get to stop to sort them out.

The grass, when we get to it, is equally fragrant with traces of all the people and dogs that have passed. And, cutting through the strong odor of sunscreen, comes the familiar scent from the day before of hamburgers, fries, hot dogs, barbecue, hot grease, and cotton candy wafting from the little trailers and tents scattered along the vast lawn. My mouth starts to water. I love these kinds of outings.

"Anyone want a Coke?" the boss asks. Both Molly and Tanya nod, but the boss, staring at a big booth with several small trailers behind it, sighs and frowns. "Quite a line." A large group of people are bunched in front of it, probably because of the delicious aroma wafting out of burgers cooking on a grill.

"Not over at that one," Molly says, pointing beyond the barbecue place to a smaller booth.

"Kettle corn?" the boss asks, in a dubious voice. "Think they'll have drinks?"

"Gotta have drinks with popcorn," Tanya says.

"And maybe we could get some to get us through to lunch?" Molly adds. "Kettle corn?" She gives the boss a wide-eyed, pleading look.

We walk over. No line except for a skinny boy who takes a handful of change from the lady behind the table and then walks away carrying two enormous bags of kettle corn, which by the smell of it, is a kind of sweet popcorn. Never had kettle corn myself, but have eaten my share of popcorn. It's good enough, but doesn't come close to being as good as burgers or barbecue. Just sayin' . . .

As the boy leaves, a tall woman turns towards us. She has a mane of white-blonde hair, kind of poofed out on top, but thinner and more straggly as it cascades down past her shoulders.

"Why look at you," the woman exclaims. She squeezes through a gap between the tables and bends over me. Up close, I can see she has bags under her eyes and deep lines cut into her tanned skin, which reminds me, somehow, of an old saddle one of my trainers used to have.

She smells of kettle corn, cookies, and some kind of perfume, one of those sweet, flowery scents.

"Ain't you just the cutest thing I seen all day?"

Cute? I don't think so. She thumps my back, and while I don't really like it, I know how to be polite. She's wearing a colorful shirt underneath one of those soft leather vests with fringe on it. Love the smell of the leather. But there's something more to her scent—I wrinkle my nostrils and sniff deeply as she continues to gush over me. Ah. Cat. That's what hiding under the heavy layer of kettle corn. More than one cat.

"What's his name?" she asks.

"Doodle," Molly says.

"Oh, that's precious. Hello, Doodle." She pats my head, which I like even less than having my back thumped. "Is he a service dog?"

The boss snorts. "Hardly."

"Bed-bug dog," Molly says.

"Oh." The lady looks impressed. "Highly trained, then."

"Yeah," the boss agrees. "At least, most of the time."

"Well, Doodle, you're so cute I could just eat you up."

I hope not! Even the boss is looking at her like she's a little crazy.

He clears his throat. "Can we get three medium Cokes? That okay?" He lifts his eyebrows at Tanya, who nods. "And—" another inquiring glance, this time at Molly "—two medium bags of kettle corn."

The woman squeezes back behind the tables and before long Molly and Tanya are munching on kettle corn, each with a drink tucked in the crook of one arm. An awkward arrangement, but one that means I get a little kettle corn myself along with bits of dirt and new grass.

We start walking, but haven't gone more than a few steps, when a wiry man with hair the color of Snippet's, but slicked back in stiff waves, calls out to us. "Beautiful dog! Standard poodle?" He's standing behind a table under another awning, with stacks of bagged dog food behind him.

"Labradoodle," Molly says. She waves at the boss who nods, and we walk over to the table. I can hardly smell the dogfood under the reek of the man's hair gel, which, frankly, does not go well with barbecue. "A bed-bug dog."

"Ah, a sniffer dog. Well a dog like that—I bet you have a pretty penny invested in him—needs a high quality food. What're you feeding him now?"

Molly says something, but I have my head under the table, away from the hair gel odor, sniffing the man's pants and shoes, which reveal he has two male dogs and a female cat. Molly tugs on the leash. "Doodle!" she says. "No. Sit." I back out and sit beside her.

"Filled with grain." The man shakes his head, his voice accusing. He has big gray eyes and a flattish nose in a reddish face mottled with freckles. "Terrible for dogs. Now TrueBites—" he waves at the shelves of bagged dog food behind him "—contains no grains. Our lamb-sweet potato mix contains everything a dog, especially a working dog like—" he peers down at me "—what's her name?"

"*His* name is Doodle," Tanya says.

"Like Diddle here. It will give him the strength and energy he needs."

"Doodle," Tanya says again, correcting him.

"Doodle. Right. And today, we have some fantastic coupons." He waves at the boss. "A great way to save money! Especially when TrueBites dog food can add years to your dog's life. And as I said, our products contain absolutely no grains whatsoever."

The boss gives him a polite nod. "How much for a twenty-five pound bag?"

"$99.95," the young man says. "But with the coup—"

"You're kidding!" the boss stares at him, incredulous.

By the expression on the man's face, he's not kidding. His freckles darken. "As I started to say, it might sound expensive, but when you factor in the fact that your dog will have fewer vet bills, more energy and a longer life, well it's the cheapest dog food on the market. It's the *best* product in the business," he says, his voice taking on an edge. "And we have two $15 off coupons to get your dog started on a lifetime of health. We can't put a price on keeping our best friends healthy, can we?"

"Er, um, thanks," the boss takes the coupons and turns resolutely away. "We have to meet someone."

After we've passed a couple of booths, the boss mutters, "I'm pretty sure I *can* put a price on it. And it's significantly less than a hundred bucks a bag."

We cross a park-like area that has picnic tables under trees. A few of the tables have people sitting around them eating, but most are empty. Then we cross a trail that runs through the park, and on the other side is the table under the pine, and behind it, the fenced-in field, set up as it was before. Except the people behind the table are different. A plump, somewhat bug-eyed woman sits next to a skinny, deeply tanned man wearing small round glasses. He has long gray hair pulled back into a ponytail.

We go up to Grady, who's waiting in front of the table, shifting his weight from one foot to the other.

"You'll both do great," Molly tells him confidently.

"I hope so." He runs a hand through his hair. "Mama's over there," Grady says, pointing to the row of seats lining the fence.

Madison stands and waves. She's wearing a wide-brimmed hat and a light-colored outfit with flowing sleeves and pants. Tanya and Molly wish Grady luck, and then we all head over to her.

"I saved you seats," she says removing a leather purse the size of a small suitcase and a bright scarf from the seats beside her. The boss sits on the furthest one, leaving the chairs nearest to Madison for Molly and Tanya.

"Miss Molly, Miss Molly," Madison says, as Molly sinks into the chair beside her, "photographer supreme!"

Molly's face flushes. "So you found a photo you can use?"

Madison reaches into a large leather purse, whisks out a piece of paper, and with a flourish hands it to Molly.

Molly looks at the check and says with astonishment, "A hundred dollars! You're using four of them?"

"Miss Molly, honey, you did a great job. I do believe you've found your calling."

Molly, still flushed with embarrassment, sticks the check into her purse. "Thanks."

"Thank *you*," Madison says, making the "you" sound a lot like Tanya's imitation in the car.

The boss looks up with interest. "Have you shown those photos to your mother?" he asks. "She might want to see them."

"I'm going to call and see if she wants them. But I figured she was too busy yesterday."

"So you haven't talked to her to see if the police have any theories?" Madison asks. "They pretty much stonewalled me when I called them."

Molly shakes her head. "Grady said it might be HEAR. That maybe they had someone throw the paint bomb at him because of the piece you did."

Madison nods. "Yeah, that ruffled some feathers, that's for sure." She gives a small, triumphant smile. "Or it could have nothing to do with the piece and they were just targeting the DogDays. They like to demonstrate at these kinds of events, like PETA does at the Westminster Dog Show. But then—" she pushes a lock of hair back under her hat "—Hailey's parents worry that maybe it was an attempted kidnapping."

"But no one tried to kidnap her," the boss points out.

"True. The Kensingtons are a little—how should I put it?— over-impressed with their own importance. As my daddy used to say, they think they're 'hot snot on a silver platter.'"

Tanya laughs loud out at this. "My granddaddy used to say that. 'You think you're hot snot on a silver platter, but you're really cold boogers on a paper plate.'"

Everyone laughs.

But then Molly says, "Tanya might have a story for you about HEAR."

Madison, suddenly alert, turns to Tanya in the way a dog might look at someone with a pocketful of really good treats. "Oh, tell me." She pulls out her phone. "Use it for notes," she says.

So Tanya repeats the story about Dan being stolen from his porch and the white van cruising the neighborhood.

"That's disturbing," the boss says vehemently. He hates stories about dogs getting lost. I've heard him say it's because he has so much money invested in me. But then he surprises me as a look of real fear passes briefly over his face. "At least it's not kids."

Madison, tapping her phone screen, says, "To some folk, their dogs *are* their kids. I'll definitely check it out. Her phone beeps and she presses a key. Suddenly, she flushes. She stares at the screen in disbelief. "I didn't think he had it in him," she says, shaking her head.

"Something wrong?" the boss asks.

"Just one of my new neighbors being a jerk. Thinks he has a God-given right to let his dog use our front yard for his waste. He objected to our method of dealing with it."

"That's rude," Tanya says indignantly.

Molly's face pales. She glances at Madison, then stares at her feet.

"Well, he'd better be richer than he looks or have a brother who's a lawyer, because he has no idea what kind of fight he just got into." Madison's thumbs move over her phone screen. "As my daddy always said, 'if you can't run with the big dogs, stay on the porch,' and I've been running with the big dogs for some time now. I think Mr. Blevins will regret the day he hired a lawyer."

"He's suing you for throwing his dog off *your* lawn?" The boss looks confused. "How can he do that?"

Molly throws Madison a panicked glance.

"It's complicated," Madison says.

"There's Grady," Molly says, a little too loudly, jabbing a finger in the direction of the field. "He's up."

Sure enough, Grady's walking onto the field, his gait stiff and his shoulders tense. Snippet dances eagerly by his side. He bends down to speak to her, and she calms down. Molly pulls out her camera.

"Oh, good. You going to film it? Then I won't have to." Madison gives Molly a distracted smile before her eyes go back to her phone. "Going to talk to a lawyer or two of my own."

We watch Grady and Snippet work their way across the field, greeting people.

"She's doing great," Tanya says at one point. Madison looks up from her phone and stares at the field a second, before saying, "Couldn't ask for better."

Snippet behaves perfectly and by the end, Grady's shoulders have relaxed. When they're done with the trial and come back through the gate, Grady pats her back and feeds her a bunch of treats.

We walk over to him and everyone congratulates Grady, although, frankly, Snippet was the one doing the work. I sit at Grady's feet, in case he wants to give out more treats, but he's too busy talking. The boss holds out a hand and Grady, beaming, shakes it. Madison, like a dog not wanting to be left out when another dog is getting petted, throws an arm around her son and gives him an awkward hug.

Then Molly checks her phone. "Almost time for us," she says to me.

And so we walk over and wait in front of the gate for our turn. As we stand there, Hailey and Hershey and Dominga come up behind us.

"Hey," Molly says politely and Hailey smiles in response, but then Molly's name is called and it's our turn to go out onto the field.

Chapter 7

Good Citizen

I SIT WHILE MOLLY GREETS A STRANGER. I LET ANOTHER stranger check my ears and paws. I stay calm when someone pulls a clanging wagon past me and when we pass through a group of people who are talking loudly. All pretty easy stuff, right?

Fortunately, today there were no intruders, either human or animal, to interrupt the test. No paint bombs either, maybe because there are lots of cops spread throughout the crowd.

Hailey and Hershey are going into the field just as we come out. "Good luck," Molly says softly, but Hailey, her eyes fixed on Hershey, doesn't respond.

We stop at the table in front of the entrance, and, after a few minutes, the ponytailed man hands Molly a sheet of paper.

Molly brandishes it in the air. "You are a Canine Good Citizen," she says, beaming. She waves it triumphantly at her dad and Tanya, who are hurrying toward her, Madison and Grady close behind.

Just as we all come together, a loud wail rises from the field. For a second, I think maybe it's another paint bomb, because the voice is Hailey's. But there's no paint bomb, just Hailey glaring at one of the judges—the one who checks the paws and ears. "You can't do that!"

The judge speaks too softly for me to understand his words, even with my excellent hearing, but when he finishes, Hailey storms off the field, Hershey trotting anxiously beside her, tail low.

Hailey marches up to the table, her face flushed and her voice indignant. "I was just doing it to give him some confidence. My trainer, Ned Gurly—you know he's *nationally* famous?—says his confidence needs building up. I don't understand why the rules forbid even a little treat. To reward him for not being scared. I just gave him *one*."

The bug-eyed woman gives a nervous giggle and then claps a hand over her mouth.

The man with the ponytail says, "The rules have to be followed by everyone." His voice is high and nasal. "No matter who trains the dogs. And the CGC rules clearly state *no treats*."

"It's a stupid rule," Hailey says.

Have to agree with her there.

The woman gives Hailey an apologetic look. "We don't make the rules, we just have to enforce them. Sorry." Another giggle escapes from her. She leans forward and says brightly, "But you're welcome to try again. We have openings—" she picks up a clipboard "—we have openings at 2:45 and at 4:10."

Hailey gives her a scathing glance. Then, with a dramatic sigh, she says, "2:45, I guess."

"I'll put you down." The woman makes a note on the clipboard. She smiles down at Hershey. "He's a handsome fellow. I bet he'll do fine without any treats."

Hailey stalks out the gate and past us without a glance in our direction, Dominga almost running to keep up.

"So she got caught," Grady says, watching her go. "Did she think the judges wouldn't notice?"

"I sure noticed it yesterday. Got it on video," Molly says. "But I wouldn't have wanted to tell on her. You know?"

Tanya and Grady both nod. But Madison raises her eyebrows. "Are you kidding? I would have given the judges that video in a hot second. I'm with the Lennon clone over there." She tilts her head towards the ponytailed man behind the table. "Rules are rules, and no matter how much money her daddy has or who he works for, she needs to abide by them."

Lennon clone? Lost me there.

Molly looks unconvinced. "I guess," she says. "I just wouldn't want to turn her in, that's all."

No one speaks for a second. Then the boss says, "So we now have two brand-new Good Citizens!" He gives Molly a big hug while Tanya throws her arms around my neck and kisses me on the nose, something I don't really like, but is okay coming from Tanya. Then the boss offers to buy barbecue for everyone.

We walk back across the park to the big circle of booths. Picnic tables and chairs are set up on the grass in the center. The boss and Grady pull two tables together under the shade of a tall pine, while Molly and Tanya get chairs. Snippet and I are both filling our noses with all the delicious smells. Literally mouth-watering.

"Eeuw. Doodle's drooling," Molly says, pulling a tissue from her purse and wiping my mouth. Hey. Can't help it.

"Give me your orders," the boss says, and after everyone—by which I mean every human—says what they want, he gets in line at the barbecue booth. "Something of everything" would be my order, if I'd been asked, except the taffy being sold a few tents down. Had that once and thought my teeth would be permanently stuck together.

Madison settles into a white chair with a sigh. "Can you believe it?" She angles her head towards a place we just passed. "Vegan dog food?" She squints. "Their sign says, 'The lamb shall lie down with the lion.'"

Grady snorts. "And then the lion eats the lamb."

Molly laughs. "Doodle, would you like to quit eating meat?"

Hah! Not until pigs fly, as an old boss liked to say, which means, according to him, "it ain't a never gonna happen." Never thought much about flying myself, but it could come in handy chasing birds and squirrels. They wouldn't be so smug then! But I'm glad pigs can't fly. That would be truly disturbing.

Madison shakes her head. "Everyone wants to make a buck from the fact that people love their pets. What will they think of next? Apple cider vinegar supplements? An all-broccoli diet? Essential oils?"

Grady crinkles his nose. "*I'd* rather eat regular dog food than an all-broccoli diet."

Me too, naturally.

The boss returns, his arms full of bags and drinks. "Who's hungry?"

Us dogs, that's who, but of course he's not talking to us. Still, I take my usual position at Molly's feet and do okay. She slips me a few fries, part of a bun, and, when the boss turns his head, a chunk of her sandwich.

Grady gives Snippet a few fries, too, but Madison catches him. "You're gonna have that dog begging whenever you eat, if you feed her from the table."

"Yes, ma'am," Grady says, putting emphasis on the ma'am in a way that makes Madison's eyes narrow briefly. But then she smiles. "I guess she deserves some treats after doing so well today. You, too." She reaches over and pats his arm. "But fries probably are as bad for her as they are for us."

Everyone talks about how well we did and how Snippet and I are good citizens, until finally, the boss stands, wipes his mouth with a napkin and starts stuffing all the trash into one bag.

Suddenly, we hear a familiar, loud wail. No need to ask whose voice it comes from.

"That girl is one hard-luck child," Madison exclaims. "Her dog must have failed again."

But then Hailey bursts out from behind the vegan tent, her face red and gasping for breath, her nanny struggling to keep up. She rushes over to our table. "Have you seen Hershey?" she asks, her voice high and shaky. "He's missing!"

Chapter 8

Hershey

"Missing!" the boss and Tanya exclaim simultaneously, their eyes wide with surprise.

"What happened?" Molly asks.

Madison slips a hand into her jacket pocket, pulls out her phone, and leans it, facing outward, against her purse on the table.

Hailey's chin trembles, and for a moment she doesn't speak. Then she takes a deep breath. "I went to the restroom and Dominga—she's my nanny—came with me. No dogs are allowed in the restrooms, so we tied Hershey's leash to the branch of this little pine tree at the edge of the entrance. Just for a second. We were hardly in there any time at all. But when we got back, he was gone. I think someone stole him."

"More likely the knot came undone," the boss says, in his let's-stay-calm voice. "I bet we'll find him if we spread out and look."

Hailey shakes her head. "I tied it really well. I don't think it could have come undone. Someone took him." Her eyes fill with tears again. "Why do they want Hershey?" she wails. "What if they hurt him?"

Tanya goes over to Hailey and gives her a hug. "It'll be okay," she says soothingly. "He's probably just lost. We'll find him."

The boss stands up. "We'll go check the concession area and see if anyone saw him."

Grady jumps to his feet. "I'll check the parking lot."

"Not alone, you won't." Madison jams her phone back in the pocket of her pants. "We'll go together. Just in case he *was* stolen, I don't want you by yourself."

Grady scowls at this, but says nothing.

The boss pulls out the little notebook and pen that he always carries in a pocket. "Can I have your number?" he asks Hailey. "In case someone sees the dog later and wants to contact you?"

Hailey turns her tear-stained face toward him. "Yeah, but my dad doesn't like me to give it out. To people I don't know. I mean you can have it, but he wouldn't want me giving it to strangers."

"Smart man," the boss agrees. He thinks a second. "If anyone wants a contact number, I'll give them my business card. And if someone calls me, I'll pass it on to you." He digs into his pocket and pulls out a handful of cards.

The boss *always* carries business cards. "If you fail to prepare, you prepare to fail," he likes to say. Not sure what he means there, except he's always ready to hand out a card to anyone who might be a potential customer.

Hailey nods eagerly. "That'll work." She rattles off a number and the boss writes it down. "We'll go search by the restrooms again and then come back here. My mom's coming and I told her we'd meet her here."

Grady and Madison head for the parking lot, while Molly, Tanya, and I follow the boss as he strides towards the booths.

"It's too bad we can't have Doodle search for him," Molly says.

"He's not trained—"

"I know," Molly interrupts. "Just bet he could find him." She's silent for a second as a man with an older, fat Rottweiler with a thick pinch collar passes us. The man's sweatshirt has cut-off sleeves, showing the tattoos that run down both his arms. My second boss, the one I don't like to think about, had tattoos like that. This man doesn't smell anything like my second boss, though, whose odor was mostly that of whiskey.

The Rottweiler walks like her paws are sore, and she's panting, tongue hanging down. Come to think of it, the sun feels a little warm on my fur. But the breeze is cool, and I certainly don't feel the need to pant. Miguel, my old trainer says fat dogs pant more because they can't handle heat well with the extra weight. He is always lecturing potential bosses on the dangers of letting their dogs get obese, which I gather means really fat.

We go first to the booth with the freckle-faced, cologne-scented man. The man's eyes light up when he see us.

"Did you decide to come back and pick up some TrueBites Premium? It will be the best decision you can make for your dog."

"Um, no." The boss shakes his head and leans forward, his voice urgent. "We're looking for a lost, or maybe stolen, dog. A chocolate Lab, named Hershey. Might have pulled loose from where he was tied. Have you seen a dog like that?"

The freckled-faced man blinks as if confused, then disappointment settles on his face. I notice, as I'm sniffing the ground around him—the cologne not being so potent there—that he's wearing old leather shoes, which are split at the toes so a bit of sock sticks out. Always love socks. I pull forward to get a better sniff, but Molly gives the leash a little tug.

"Chocolate Lab? Probably seen five or six of them today. Popular breed. None of them without an owner, though." The man brightens. "One lady with chocolate Lab bought a four-month supply of our premium blend."

The boss hands the man one of his cards. "If a dog with a leash dragging comes by, would you grab it and give me a call?"

The freckled man takes the card, glances at it and looks up at the boss with sudden interest. "Is there a reward?"

"Maybe," the boss says. "Just let me know if you see a brown Lab."

"You sure you don't want a bag of dog food while you're here?"

"Sorry," the boss says. He turns away and pulls out his phone. "This is going to take a while," he says. "I told Barbara I'd have you girls back by four."

"We could split up," Molly offers. "It'll go faster. Tanya and I could start with the vegan booth and work our way around. Meet in the middle."

"That'll work. But stay in sight." The boss gives Molly some cards to hand out.

We cross the open area, and come to a table where a cheerful girl who doesn't look much older than Molly gives us a welcoming smile. She's wearing tight jeans and sandals that have sparkly stones in them. Her hair, long and blonde, reaches to the middle of her back, held by a silky bow.

"Hey," Tanya says quickly, just as the blonde girl starts to speak, "We're looking for a lost or maybe stolen dog."

"A chocolate Lab named Hershey," Molly adds. "He might be running loose dangling a leash."

"Really?" The girl's brow creases. "I've seen several chocolate Labs today, and about a million black Labs, but no loose dogs. How long ago?"

"Maybe ten, fifteen minutes?" Molly says. "We're not exactly sure."

The girl shakes her head, and then waves at another girl coming toward us carrying a paper sack and a couple of drinks. I lift my nose toward the sack, expecting to smell barbecue, but sadly it's just salad.

The new girl goes around to the back and enters the booth. She's wearing thick sandals without any shiny stones, baggy cotton pants, and a faded t-shirt that has writing on the front. Her hair is a mop of tangled curls that looks like it needs a visit to the groomer. Her sweaty face is flushed and bumpy with pimples.

"Hey, Suzanne. Someone lost a dog. A chocolate Lab."

Suzanne sets the drinks on the table, then pulling two Styrofoam containers from the bag as the blonde girl repeats what Molly told her. She shakes her head. "Haven't seen a dog like that."

Molly says, "Okay, thanks." She turns to go, but Tanya, her eyes on the bags of dogfood, says, "Anyone really buy vegan dog food?"

Suzanne bristles like a terrier who has just heard an intruder. "If we can't learn to live without violence there is no hope for this planet," she declares. "Our dogfood has all the protein and nutrition that a dog needs for a healthy active life. And it's all from plant-based foods harvested in a fully sustainable way." She glares at Tanya as if daring her to disagree.

Tanya seems unimpressed.

And Molly as well. "Sustainable maybe but not natural. I mean, dogs and meat . . ." Molly shrugs, smiling.

But Suzanne scowls. "The reason we humans have our big brains is hopefully to solve the real problems in the world. And cruelty to animals in one of those things. But you wouldn't understand that, you with your designer dog that you enslave."

Whoa. Suzanne's voice is suddenly so angry my own hackles rise.

Molly takes a step back, the color rushing to her face.

"Suzanne," the blonde girl says in a low voice. "Honey and vinegar, remember?" A truly baffling statement, but Suzanne grimaces and says in a fierce voice, "I'm going to the restroom."

"Sorry," the blonde girl says, as we watch Suzanne stride away. "She gets a little intense. For me, this is just a job and some extra money, but for Suzanne it's this big philosophy, you know? Our manager keeps telling her we'll catch more flies with honey than vinegar." At this, she laughs, picks up a small bag and with a wink asks, "Can I interest you in a free sample?"

Molly's shoulders relax and she smiles back. "Thanks, but I don't think Doodle wants to be a vegan. But—" she digs out one of the boss's cards from her pocket and hands it to her. "If you do see a loose dog, this is my dad's number."

The blonde girl scans the card. "Bed bugs?" she says, laughing. "Wonder if Suzanne feels *they* have a right to life. I know I don't!"

We leave the vegan place and stop at a bunch of other booths, but no one has seen Hershey. When we return to the picnic area, Hailey is sitting on a bench, looking distraught as usual. Grady and Madison are still gone. But Mario has shown up and is talking to Dominga, who listens for a bit and then hands him some money.

"What time does the movie end?" Dominga asks, as the boy pockets the cash. She speaks with Spanish accent much like my old trainer, Miguel.

"Six or six-thirty," Mario replies.

"Come straight home," Dominga says.

The boy nods and takes off at a jog toward the parking lot.

Hailey's eyebrows raise as she turns to the boss. "Hershey?"

The boss shakes his head. "No one we talked to saw any sign of him."

No surprise there. There wasn't a trace of Hershey's scent at any of the booths we stopped out. There are tiny whiffs of his scent here, though, probably from Hailey, although I'm not close enough to be sure.

Hailey says, "He has to be stolen. Otherwise we would have found him. Why would someone take him? He's microchipped, so they couldn't show him."

No one speaks for a moment.

And then, from the direction of the parking lot, a woman strides purposely towards us, head high. She waves and calls Hailey's name, and I suddenly recognize her—the woman who hugged Hailey after the paint bombs. She's wearing form-fitting pants that tuck into her knee high boots, and a blazer over a button-down shirt. I work my nose, catching a faint smell of perfume, and, even fainter, of Hershey.

"My mother," Hailey says, not looking especially excited to see her.

Dominga, who had just sat down beside Hailey, immediately gets up and moves to the other side of the picnic table. Hailey gives her a plaintive look, then, with a small sigh, turns to face her mother, who rushes straight up to her and, once again, pulls her into a stiff hug.

"What a mess," Hailey's mother says, releasing her. "I don't understand who would do such a thing, just take a dog who obviously belongs to someone. I've talked to the police—had to play phone tag for almost twenty minutes before I got the desk sergeant in charge of this area."

Phone tag? Sounds interesting. I can pretty much beat anyone at regular tag because I'm so fast no one can ever catch me. Like keep-away, tag is one of my favorite games. But I've never played it with phones. In my experience, people never allow dogs to touch their phones.

"—our taxes for this kind of incompetence," Hailey's mother is saying. She turns a questioning gaze over to the table where the boss, Molly, Tanya and I are sitting and raises an eyebrow at Hailey.

"These are my, um, friends," Hailey says. She points at Molly and Tanya. She gives them an apologetic shrug. "Sorry. Can't remember your names." And then, to her mother, "They go to my school. And they all helped search for Hershey."

The boss, with a friendly nod toward Hailey's mother, puts a hand on Molly's shoulder. "This is Molly, and—" he gestures at Tanya "—Tanya. They're both in Ms. Mandisa's class. And I'm Josh Hunter, Molly's father."

"Brooke Kensington," the woman replies in a cool voice. "I appreciate your taking the time to help my daughter." Despite her words, she seems more annoyed than appreciative.

Hailey sinks back down onto the bench, twisting her hands in an agitated manner.

And then, Madison and Grady return, Snippet leading the way, tugging at the end of the leash.

"No luck," Grady says, a little breathlessly, as Snippet tows him over to where she can sniff noses with me. He gives the leash a little jerk. "She's forgotten how to be a good citizen," he says in a low voice, grimacing at Molly. "Pulled the whole way back here."

And then, to Hailey, "Only dogs we saw were a boxer and two collies. No Labs of any color."

Madison's eyes widen slightly at the sight of Mrs. Kensington, and her hand slips into her jacket pocket. "You must be Hailey's mama," she says, walking up to her. "What a terrible thing to have happen to your poor baby girl. I just can't believe all the drama we've had at this dog show. It's worse than a rock concert." She extends a hand, smiling. "I'm Madison Greene. My son Grady is in Hailey's class."

Mrs. Kensington, frowning slightly, does not take the outstretched hand. "Madison Greene? That blog person?"

Madison beams at her. "Guilty as charged, I'm afraid." She gives a little laugh.

Mrs. Kensington's frown deepens. "We do not want this . . . this situation on any blog," she says in severe voice. "Is that understood?"

"Yes, ma'am," Madison says with a thicker than normal accent, a smile still plastered on her face, but her eyes now angry. "Anything us po' folk can do to help."

Mrs. Kensington stares at her a second, and then, with a heavy sigh, "I'm sorry. I didn't mean to be rude. All of this has been extremely . . . upsetting. First the paint bombs, and now Hershey. . . . And it's all coming at a difficult time." She sticks out her hand. "Brooke Kensington."

Madison takes it, her eyes softening a bit, but the smile gone.

"I'm sure you understand our need for privacy." Mrs. Kensington says, in a firm voice.

Madison answers this with a short nod.

"So," Mrs. Kensington says, in a take-charge manner, "Hailey, can you tell me again exactly what happened?"

Hailey recounts the story, sniffling at bit, but for once without any tears or wailing.

When she's finished, Mrs. Kensington turns a critical eye to Dominga. "I don't think I understand why you didn't stay out and hold Hershey. When you knew how important he is to my daughter."

Hailey shoots a startled look at her mother, while Dominga blinks in surprise. "The dog," she says, "we did not think . . . we were so quick. I'm so sorry."

"You're being paid to think"—Mrs. Kensington regards Dominga, her eyes cold and her voice hard—"not to be sorry. Your job is to *protect* my daughter and help to keep her and the things she loves safe. That's why we entrusted her into your care."

Hailey gasps, pushing her hair back from her face, then twisting her hands on her lap as her gaze shifts anxiously from her mother to Dominga and back again.

"But that is why I always go with your daughter into the restrooms. So she is safe,"

"Mo-om," Hailey cries out. "She *was* trying to protect me. It isn't her fault. You're always blaming her for everything, when it's not her fault. She takes perfect care of me all the time, which you wouldn't know because you're never around." She jumps up, crying, and runs over to Dominga, burying her head against the nanny's chest. Dominga pats her back, but the look she gives Mrs. Kensington is full of dismay, maybe because Hailey's mother's face has turned red and the scent of anger pours from her now rigid body.

"You. Will. Not. Talk. To. Me. That. Way." Mrs. Kensington says to her daughter, each word filled with cold fury. She turns to Dominga. "I can take my daughter home. You are no longer needed here."

"No," wails Hailey. "I don't want her to go."

Mrs. Kensington keeps her eyes fixed on Dominga, who reluctantly extracts herself from Hailey and stands. "Yes, Mrs. Kensington." She hesitates, then in an earnest, half-pleading tone says, "She does not mean what she is saying. About you. She is upset about the dog. That is all."

Mrs. Kensington draws herself up, her expression so fierce it makes my hackles rise. "I do not need you to tell me what my daughter thinks and feels, thank you very much. I am her *mother.*"

Dominga gives a brief nod, and, eyes, downcast, she picks up her bag and walks towards the parking lot. Hailey sobs as she watches her go.

No one speaks after that for a long time. Finally, the boss checks his phone. "We need to get going. Barbara will wonder what's happened to us."

Molly nods, her face pale. She looks near tears herself.

Madison jumps up. "Yes, I've got a blog to do."

Neither Mrs. Kensington nor Hailey look in our direction, when we start walking toward the parking lot.

"Don't bother to say goodbye or thanks for all the help," Madison murmurs. "Piece of work." And then, when we get to the blacktop, "That baby girl has more problems than her lost dog. Sad."

"What do you mean?" Grady asks.

"She's about to lose her nanny." She shakes her head. "She ought to know that the first rule for keeping nannies is to never let the parents know how much you love them."

"I'm afraid you're right," the boss says. "Did you see the look on her mother's face?"

"Dragon lady," Grady says. "Wouldn't want to live with her to save my life."

For some reason, this seems to make Madison happy. She smiles down at her son.

We come to the van and, after a few goodbyes, Molly puts me in my crate and sits beside Tanya in the back seat like before.

And then the boss turns on the radio, and, like the man on the boss's country music station is singing, we're rolling down the highway.

Chapter 9

Blind Dan

WHEN WE PULL UP TO TANYA'S DRIVEWAY, MOLLY gets out with Tanya, and opens my crate, and then— not sure how I missed this earlier—she gets her backpack from the front seat. Not her school backpack, but the one she uses as a suitcase. Turns out Molly's going to spend the night at the Franklin's. And, of course, I'm invited, too, because after the thing with Kenny, Tanya's brother—long story—Mrs. Franklin says I can stay with her any time day or night.

Apparently the boss doesn't remember this. When Mrs. Franklin answers the door, he says, "Thanks for doing this. You sure Doodle won't be too much trouble?"

Mrs. Franklin is as tall as the boss, but much wider. She's wearing an apron and her hands smell like sugar and flour. "Isn't he now a *cer*-ti-fied good citizen?" she asks, smiling.

"Well," the boss says, "I wouldn't count on it." But he's smiling as well.

"You and Annie just have a good time," she says, waving him off. "Everyone needs a night out sometime."

I follow the girls back to Tanya's bedroom. Although they have a smaller yard than we do—believe me, an issue when finding a place to pee—the Franklin's house is actually bigger. They have three bedrooms on the main floor, which are used by Tanya, her little brother Tyson, and Mr. and Mrs. Franklin. Then, in the basement, there's a shop/storage area that smells like mildew and also like motor oil, because Mr. Franklin is a mechanic and always has some project laid out on a work-bench. There are two small bedrooms downstairs that Tanya's older brothers, Kenny and Derrin use, plus a tiny bathroom that has only a sink and a toilet.

Molly drops her backpack under Tanya's desk and Tanya shuts the door. The girls sit cross-legged on the bed while I stretch out on the floor.

Soon, they're talking a mile a minute again, about Hershey, about how Hailey is, in Tanya's words, "too full of herself," and how Hailey's mother is, again in Tanya's words, "an ice queen."

After a while, Mrs. Franklin knocks at the door. "Cake's ready," she says. We follow her to the kitchen where she hands Tanya a long pan full of cake. Mrs. Franklin calls these sheet cakes, which has nothing to do with the kind of sheets that go on beds, in case you were wondering. This one smells like sugar, oil, cin-namon, and apples.

"—and tell them we're truly sorry about Dan," Mrs. Franklin is saying. "And don't be too long—I know how Peggy can talk—'cause dinner's in an hour."

Tanya picks up the cake. "We're going to take this to the Cart-ers," she tells Molly.

Molly runs back to the bedroom to grab my leash and no-pull harness and soon we're off, walking down the sidewalk, Tanya carrying the cake.

She turns down the first crossroad and then about half a block later, into the driveway of a small house with dull gray wood siding. A porch spans the full width of the house, and half the porch is screened in. We go up the steps and Molly rings the doorbell.

After a few moments and the sound of heavy footsteps on the other side, the door opens. The first thing I see is an enormous expanse of yellow, which turns out to be a cottony flowing blouse of a woman who is much broader than Mrs. Franklin, but nowhere near as tall. Her hair, as curly as my own, forms a cap of tight white curls on her head, like Mr. Franklin's, although his hair is even shorter. She's wearing fluffy slippers that have a faint mildew odor.

"Why, Tanya, good to see you!" The woman smiles, then looks at Molly. "And who is this pretty young lady?"

"Hey, Mrs. Carter." Tanya grins back at her. "This is Molly Hunter. And her dog, Doodle. He's a bed-bug dog."

"Oh, Doodle, yes. I saw that blog about him—the one you were in. You're a TV star." She winks at Tanya. And then to Molly, "Pleased to meet you, Miss Molly."

Tanya thrusts the cake forward. "Mama sent this cake for you. It's her apple cake. She says it's your favorite."

"Your mama is a great woman. Of course," Mrs. Carter pats her considerable stomach, "I need cake like I need a hole in the head." In spite of her words, she takes the cake happily. "Come in and visit a second."

Tanya explains that we can't stay. Molly walks over to the screened-in section of the porch. "Is this where Dan, um, was taken from?"

At the mention of Dan, the smile leaves Mrs. Carter's face. "You heard about him? Yes, that's where he was, poor baby. Suddenly, her eyes well with tears and she looks down at the cake in her hands as if she doesn't know what to do with it.

"Can I go put that in the kitchen for you?" Tanya asks.

"Sorry," Mrs. Carter says. "Yes, thank you." She pushes the pan into Tanya's arms, then tugs a tissue from a pocket. Wiping her eyes, she says, "We can't figure out how he got out. Try the door."

Molly tries to turn the handle on the door, but it won't turn.

"That's how we left it. Just like that. I *always*—" her voice breaks and she swallows. "I always jiggle it to make sure it's locked. Every time."

"How do you open it?" Molly asks.

Tanya, back from delivering the cake, says, "That little latch on the side there? Push it up."

Molly does so and pulls open the door. "So anyone could have opened it and let him out?" she asks.

"But why would anyone do that? Everyone in the neighborhood knows Dan. No one would let him out. He's a good dog. Doesn't bark a lot, like some Jack Russells." Her eyes well up and she dabs the now-soggy tissue at them. Tanya and Molly exchange a look.

"I'm sorry," Mrs. Carter says. "I just miss him so much. We got him from that pet store over on South Arlington Mill, which I know we shouldn't have. He was such a cute puppy. But then he developed something called lens luxation, which the vet told us Jack Russells are prone to if the breeders aren't careful. Told us pet store dogs often aren't healthy. But we didn't know, and by then we loved him. Poor dog was in so much pain that we paid to have his eyes removed."

Molly's face goes pale. "His eyes removed?"

Tanya says, "Sounds gross, but he looked fine afterward, right Mrs. Carter? He just looked like his eyes were closed all the time."

"And he got around fine," Mrs. Carter says, nodding. "Cost a fortune. We'd saved the money for one of those cruises they're always advertising on TV, but Dan needed it more. He was such an affectionate boy. Would takes turns sitting on our laps while we watched TV. And we were glad we did the surgery. He was so much happier after that. No more pain and he did well, quickly learned where every piece of furniture was. But now—" her face sags, and her eyes take on a hopeless expression "—now he's gone."

"We'll keep looking," Tanya says, touching Mrs. Carter's arm. "Maybe he'll turn up."

"Have you checked all the shelters?" Molly asks. "When Doodle was lost, he ended up in a shelter in a different county."

Hey, I remember that. Not the best time of my life, that's for sure.

"I call all the shelters in the area every day," Mrs. Carter says. "They're tired of my voice. But I don't want him to slip through any cracks. Don't want him to get put down because some clerk forgot to make a note."

"Sometimes shelters have Facebook pages for lost dogs. I saw some when we were looking for Doodle," Molly says.

Mrs. Carter looks doubtful. "I don't do that Facebook thing myself . . ."

"You don't need to," Molly assures her. "I could email the shelters. Do you have any pictures of him? We could make some posters."

Mrs. Carter brightens, grinning down at Molly. "Honey, I got drawers full of them. Just a minute." She disappears through the front door, and comes back before long and hands Molly a short stack of photos.

"I don't need them back. Got copies of all of them when they had that two-for-one down at Kroger's."

Molly quickly looks through the photos. "Thanks. This will be great!"

Tanya says, "We gotta go. Promised we'd be home for dinner."

Mrs. Carter nods and tells Tanya to be sure and thank her mother for the cake and, with lots of goodbyes, we head back to Tanya's.

"Poor Mrs. Carter," Molly says, when we turn back onto Tanya's street.

Tanya agrees. "I bet those HEAR people took him. Who'd steal a blind dog? You couldn't sell him."

A surge of tension goes through Molly's hand right through the leash. "Or dog fighters. I've heard they steal them for . . ." She hesitates as if reluctant to say the word. "Bait."

"Dog fighters are the scum of the earth," Tanya says hotly, "and Mama says she hopes they have a special place in hell reserved for them." She pauses a second. "But we haven't had that problem around here. I think Derrin or Kenny would know. They hear about everything."

"We could put up signs," Molly says. "Posters."

Tanya says, "What about Grady's mom? Maybe she'd do a piece on Dan. Like Gunther."

Gunther is a German shepherd who used to be a bed-bug dog but had a bunch of problems and is now retired. He was lost for a while, too.

"Great idea," Molly says, just as we're walking up the steps to Tanya's door.

Dinner turns out to be make-your-own-sandwich night, because Mrs. Franklin had to work and then make the cake, and because Mr. Franklin and Tanya's brothers are all at a game. Sadly, for once, Molly eats all of her sandwich. She also polishes off a fair-sized mound of what Mrs. Franklin calls her world-famous coleslaw. Famous or not, I can say from previous experience that coleslaw suffers from being mostly cabbage, a substance not really considered a food in the dog world. So I don't mind that no one offers me any. I'll take kibble over cabbage any day, which is good, since that's what I end up with tonight.

After dinner, Tanya asks her mother for poster paper.

Mrs. Franklin frowns. "Why do you want that?"

"To make lost dog posters. To help Mrs. Carter find Dan," Molly says.

"She gave us pictures of him to use," Tanya adds. "She really misses him."

Mrs. Franklin's eyes darken. "I know, baby. But the chance of finding him . . . I'm pretty sure that dog is long gone. I hope you didn't make her think you'd find him. Nothing worse than pining for something that ain't never gonna be, as my mama used to say."

Molly says earnestly, "We didn't promise her anything except we'd help get the word out. Just in case."

But Mrs. Franklin shakes her head sadly. "*Just in case*? Honey, those words *drip* hope."

Molly looks stricken. "But what if Dan is somewhere and doesn't ever get home because no one tries to find him?" she asks. "We have to try."

"We *gotta* try," Tanya echoes.

Mrs. Franklin sighs, slowly shaking her head. "Well, we haven't had poster paper in the house since Tyson's last science project."

"Okay," Tanya says in a discouraged voice. I follow her and Molly to her room, where the girls perch on the bed, neither speaking.

"What about flyers?" Tanya says after a while. "We could put them in the mail boxes."

Molly's face lights up. "That's even better! No one really looks at posters much anyway. My dad has a scanner. I could scan in the photos to use." Then her eyes narrow. "He only has a black and white printer, though."

"We have a color one," Tanya says. "You can make the flyers then print them here." She jumps off the bed and gets a pen and a notebook. "What should we say?"

I don't find out, because somehow, full stomach and all, I drift off.

Chapter 10

Uncle Armando's Surprise

THE NEXT DAY, AFTER CHURCH, MRS. FRANKLIN CALLS the boss and offers to drop Molly and me off on her way to pick up Mr. Franklin's mother, who lives at Serenity Falls Retirement Home, a place the boss and I visit sometimes to check for bed bugs.

"Unless you'd like to come over for dinner," Mrs. Franklin says. "You know you're always invited."

The boss thanks her, but says we've all had such a busy weekend, we need some down time, which doesn't mean he has to be in a "down/stay" like it sometimes does for dogs.

So Mrs. Franklin lets us off at the curb. From the house comes the sound of guitar and a low voice singing. I assume the boss is playing his country music on the radio. To my surprise—and Molly's, too, by the way her eyebrows shoot up—the music comes from the boss himself. He's sitting on the couch strumming a guitar. The house smells of chicken, cream cheese, and onion, a mouth-watering aroma that means the boss has cooked his favorite crockpot chicken dish.

His face lights up in that way it so often does when he sees Molly. "How'd it go?" he says. "Was Doodle good?"

As if he needed to ask!

"Doodle was great." Molly looks at the guitar. "You haven't played in ages!"

"Yeah. Got it out last night. I was telling Annie how your mother and I were in a band when we were in high school, and Annie said she plays as well, so we spent the evening going through songs."

"Mom played in a band?" Molly stares at him wide-eyed.

"You didn't know that?"

Molly shakes her head.

The boss seems surprised. Not sure why, since there are lots of things about her mother that Molly doesn't know. "She played keyboard and I played guitar." He laughs, his eyes soft with memory. "I bet we were awful—the band, I mean—but we had fun, and your mother had a lovely voice. Probably still does." He sighs, then gets up and lays the guitar in its case. "And Annie does, too."

"Will you teach me to play?"

The boss hesitates for a moment, then says, "Sure. Not right now, because dinner's almost done. But, yeah."

Molly freezes for a second. "I almost forgot!" She runs to her bedroom and returns carrying several sheets of paper. "This is for orchestra. We're going to get our instruments next week so we can learn to use them and then we can have practices in the summer."

She hands the papers to the boss. He scans them. "Oboe?" he says dubiously. "That's a little . . . exotic."

"Ms. Stenson—she's the music director—says oboe would be good because flute players and drummers are a dime a dozen. Those are the instruments everyone picks. And I'll have more chances to play if I pick oboe. Same with strings, she says. It's better to pick viola than violin. But I don't want to do viola."

"But an oboe . . . flutes are probably cheaper . . ." the boss studies the papers, frowning.

"Ms. Stenson says we can rent one as cheaply as a flute," Molly says. "Plus, she played one for our class and I really like the way they sound. Kind of, I don't know, mysterious."

The boss sighs and says, "I'll fill it out after dinner." He shakes his head. "Oboe!"

We follow him into the kitchen, where, just as I thought, the crockpot sits, sweating a little, and emitting glorious scents. The boss puts a pan of water on the stove, and when it starts to boil, dumps part of a package of noodles into it. He whistles softly as he slices a cucumber, then sweeps up the slices and drops them in a clear salad bowl, already mostly full.

Molly puts plates and silverware on the table and puts ice in a couple of glasses.

Before long, he and Molly are eating salad and the chicken dish over buttered noodles. Molly doesn't usually give me any of this dish, because it has lots of onion and garlic, which she thinks is bad for dogs. As I've probably mentioned before, I have my doubts. It certainly doesn't *smell* bad for me.

Molly tells the boss about blind Dan and the visit to Mrs. Carter. "I got photos of him that we can scan and send to the Jack Russell rescue places. She called a bunch of them, and they told her they'll make sure the photos will go out to all the shelters. Plus Tanya and I are going to make flyers."

"Sounds good," the boss says, taking a sip of diet ginger ale, his favorite drink for reasons I can't understand, but must have nothing to do with taste. "Although if he's been gone over a week . . ."

Molly sets down her fork. "I know," she says glumly. "That's what Mrs. Franklin says." Then, brightening, "But maybe if we could get Madison to do a story on him, he'll get found. Like Gunther."

The boss considers this. "Maybe. If something hasn't happened to him already." He takes a bite of noodles and chicken. "But only if Madison's interested in the story on her own. I don't want her doing favors for us. I don't want to owe her anything, you know?"

Molly doesn't look like she knows at all. But she swallows a bite of salad and says, "I'll talk to Grady. He can give her the idea, and if she wants to use it, she can."

So, later, after Molly and the boss have cleaned up the kitchen and I've had my after-dinner pee, Molly and the boss settle on the couch, and I curl down on my bed by Molly's feet. Over Christmas, the boss learned how to view computer stuff on the big TV in the living room, and now that's where they like to watch things like Madison's blog. Much better than crowding around his laptop in the bedroom, like they used to do.

Soon I hear the familiar music, and then Madison's face fills the screen. "Hi, y'all. Welcome to the *States of Affairs* newscast, *The Low Down News*. Bringing you the low down to stories important to Northern Virginia.

"A series of criminal acts marred the DogDays this weekend at Saratoga Park in Arlington. On Friday evening, the Canine Good Citizen test proved unexpectedly colorful when someone tossed two paint bombs into the testing arena."

"Hey, that's my photo," Molly says.

"—no one was hurt."

"And another of mine!" Molly shouts, while Madison explains what the dog/handler teams have to do to pass the Good Citizen test.

"Good shot," the boss says, and Molly smiles.

"—no one has come forward to admit throwing the paint bombs, and police are still investigating. There are rumors—" Madison leans forward, her face earnest—"and I repeat, they are currently only rumors, that Humanitarians for Enlightened Animal Relations, or HEAR, might be behind the attack. Certainly, it is the type of thing that HEAR has done at other dog events, which the *Low Down News* covered in our January 21st broadcast, available on our website. HEAR has not responded to our attempts to contact them."

The screen changes to a picture of the park. Hey, there's the barbecue place!

"And then, on Saturday afternoon, a twelve-year-old girl left her dog, a chocolate Lab, briefly tied up by the entrance to the women's restroom and came out to find the dog gone, presumably stolen."

Hailey's face comes on the screen. Red-eyed and puffy-faced, her cheeks shine with tears.

"Hailey Kensington, daughter of Roderick and Brooke Kensington of Arlington, had her precious puppy, Hershey, taken from her. Hershey is a seven-month old chocolate Labrador retriever."

"How on earth did she get that photo?" the boss asks.

"I don't know," Molly says. "On her phone maybe?"

Madison keeps talking, but somehow I drift off to sleep.

Later, Molly and I are in her room, her on the computer and me continuing my nap, when her voice wakes me up.

"Hey, Grady." She's talking into her phone. "I found out more about that dog that went missing in Tanya's neighborhood. That Jack Russell?"

"Yeah?"

"Tanya and I visited Mrs. Carter—remember her neighbor with the blind dog stolen off the porch?"

"You thought it might be HEAR, right? Does she know for sure it was stolen?"

"She says the door to the screened in porch was latched when she came home. If he'd somehow got out by himself, it'd be open."

"Makes sense," Grady says. "But she's old, right? She might have left it open and forgotten about it."

"I don't think so," Molly says. "And, if she did, it'd still be open, not latched. Anyway, I wonder if your mom might do a piece on Dan—so people will look for him like they did with Gunther. Mrs. Carter really misses him. She can't talk about him without crying."

"I don't know." Grady's voice takes on an edge. "I never can tell what she's going to be interested in. You can ask her . . . wait a sec . . ."

Molly frowns, while the sound of muffled voices comes through her phone. And then Madison's voice, loud and clear says, "Hey, Molly. You might have a story?"

"Yeah. Tanya and I visited her neighbor, the one with the missing dog." She repeats what she told Grady, including how the gate was latched and ending with how much Mrs. Carter misses Dan. She clears her throat, and her words speed up. "I was wondering if you could do a piece on him, and say that HEAR is suspected, and anyone with any information could come forward. So that if HEAR has him, maybe they'll let him go. And if they don't, maybe someone's seen him and will call in, like with Gunther."

"I can't go on the air saying the dog was stolen with no proof whatsoever. Why do you think HEAR did it?"

"Tanya says one of the neighbors saw their van in the area the same day."

"I'd need to know which neighbor and exactly what time the van was seen. And, really, I'd rather have two or three witnesses. Or ten." She sighs. "And even if you find people who'll say they saw the van in the area, that's still not proof that HEAR stole the dog. Now if I had someone who actually saw them on the Carters' porch . . ."

Madison pauses for a second, then says, "Sorry, Molly. *States of Affairs* gives me some leeway, but they don't have endless resources for legal fees, especially if it looks like I'm creating stories out of thin air."

"But you said HEAR was suspected for the paint bombs," Molly says in a stubborn voice. "On your blog."

"And I have a quote from a police investigator to back it up."

Molly's shoulders sag and for a moment she doesn't speak. "Could you maybe just post his picture as a lost dog and see if anyone's found him?"

Madison says in an irritated voice, "Maybe I should just give up investigative reporting and make my blog a lost and found service for dogs."

"Mama," Grady's voice says in the background, sounding upset.

Molly mumbles, "Sorry."

"No problem," Madison says briskly. "And if you find out anything more . . . concrete . . . I'd definitely be interested."

Molly says goodbye, and sits slumped in front of her computer, not moving. After a while, her phone starts to vibrate and play its music.

"Who's—" she says staring at the screen, and then in a tentative voice, "Hello?"

"Is this la Señorita María Maureen Hunter, *detectiva suprema*?" The man's deep voice comes through the phone's speaker. He says the words with an exaggerated Spanish accent, which I know is fake because I remember that voice well and it usually just has a trace of accent.

Molly squeals with delight. "Uncle Armando!"

Hearing him brings to mind the faint scent of men's cologne, and stronger ones of enchiladas, garlic, and chilies. I can almost see the man with his graying hair, trim moustache, and smiling black eyes. Suddenly I wish we could go to his restaurant, Los Dos Amigos. Great food there, but it turns out to be far away, up in the mountains.

According to Molly, he's not really her uncle, but her mother's first cousin. No idea what she means by that, or even what an aunt or uncle is, frankly, except for some kind of relative, usually older, which fits, because Armando is quite a bit older than Molly's mother. Dogs don't go into relationships the way that humans do.

Molly frowns, suddenly worried, "Is everyone okay?"

"Fine. Perfect. I'm calling because—do you know about the big demonstration coming up? Keep Our Children Home?"

"Keep Our Children Home?" Molly repeats, looking puzzled.

"It's a Latino organization that works to keep children who are U.S. citizens, but whose parents are illegal immigrants, from being deported. As you can imagine, it's a subject near to our hearts. Mariela and I are coming to DC to join the protest."

"I hadn't heard about it. Protesting? Like what happened to Mom?"

Armando says, "Exactly, like that." His voice turns hard. "Fifteen years later and they're still sending kids who've grown up their whole lives here back to Mexico or Honduras or Guatemala where they're complete strangers to the culture. Kids on track teams and chess clubs. Sometimes kids who don't even speak Spanish. Makes me angry to think about it. Your mother was the exception, you know, not leaving."

"'Cause she got married," Molly says. "Dad says she probably wouldn't have married him if she hadn't had to do it to stay here." Whoa. Her voice catches, her eyes suddenly moist. I get up and touch my nose to her hand, and she clenches a fist into my fur.

"Well, he can't know that," Armando says. "At the time, she was very much in love with him, as he was with her. It didn't hurt that marrying him helped her to stay here, but I think they would have married anyway."

Molly swallows. "Sorry," she gulps.

For a moment, no one speaks. "Don't take your father's words too seriously," Armando says at last, in a gentle tone. "People tend to reimagine history after a divorce. Remember, I was there. In the center of it all: Cori's parents furious with her and with Josh, his parents scandalized that their son was marrying a Mexican, and your parents, like all young people in love, headstrong and defiant."

"Marmie says she and GrandJum didn't care that Mom was Mexican, but that my dad was so young."

Marmie and GrandJum, Molly's grandparents, are wonderful people who have this great place in the mountains, not too far from Los Dos Amigos. Molly and I had quite an adventure there once, although it's not something I'd like to have happen again.

"Well," Armando pauses. "Maybe I'm wrong about that." He sighs. "But, back to the demonstration. It's going to run on Saturday and Sunday, the 19th and 20th. We thought we'd come up a few days early and do some sightseeing. We have to go back Sunday, but we'll be at the demonstration on Saturday. My son, Rodrigo—you haven't met him yet—just got a job in DC and is in the process of moving his family to Arlington. And my youngest daughter, Silvia, will be renting from him. She's an attorney there. So you will have relatives almost within spitting distance."

"That's great." Molly's sadness vanishes. "Are you staying with Rodrigo? I could ask Dad about having you come here."

"Rodrigo hasn't had time to unpack. But we already have a place to stay, better than the finest hotel in D.C. and much less costly."

"Where?" Molly asks, baffled.

"At *La Casa Corazón*."

"You're staying with *Mom*?" She goes from baffled to delighted. "That's *great*! That's . . ." She seems stumped for words.

"First time I will have seen her since she left Laurel Woods. And you know you had something to do with that."

Not sure what Armando means, but Molly's head moves in a slight nod.

They talk some more, Armando filling her in on what's been happening with the rest of the family.

After he says goodbye, Molly rushes into the living room, and begins to repeat to the boss everything Armando told her.

"Did you know about it?" she asks, after telling him about the demonstration.

The boss shakes his head.

"Can we go?" Her face takes on the expression of a puppy begging for a treat. "It's important. And it's all about Mom."

The boss rubs his beard, frowning a little.

"If you don't want to go, I could probably go with Uncle Armando. Or Mom."

"Probably," he says. "As long as it's not supposed to be dangerous."

"Dangerous?" She looks at him as if he might be crazy. "Great!" she says, heading back towards her room.

The boss mutters, "That wasn't exactly a yes," but Molly doesn't seem to hear. She already has her phone to her ear.

"Hey, Tanya?" she says. "Guess what?"

Nothing I haven't heard before, which means it's time for me to curl down on the rug beside her and take a nap.

Chapter 11

Breaking the Law

MORE GOOD NEWS! WHEN THE BOSS PICKS UP MOLLY after school, he picks up Tanya as well and announces they're going to the Franklin's.

"Doodle, too?" Molly asks, always looking out for me.

The boss smiles. "Barbara said it'd be fine."

What Mrs. Franklin really said was, "Why do you bother to ask? You know I'll take that dog any day of the week."

The boss adds, "I have to stop by the DMV, and if there's time, I'm going to get a haircut. This way Doodle won't have to be in his crate all afternoon."

Never been sure what the DMV is, but I know the boss hates it almost as much as he hates traffic, and is usually grumpy when he returns from there, so I'm extra happy to be with Molly.

The boss drops us off, and, after the girls get a snack, we all go to Tanya's room. Molly digs a stack of papers from her backpack, and holds up a single sheet. "In half or thirds?" she asks.

"Thirds look more letter-like," Tanya says. So they divide up the stack and fold every sheet, then put them back in Molly's backpack. Molly puts on my harness.

"We're going to take Doodle on a walk," Tanya tells her mother, who's in the kitchen. Both she and Molly seem a little nervous, but Mrs. Franklin doesn't notice.

"Okay. Josh said he'd be back about five, so don't be too long," she says, her eyes a little watery from the onions she's chopping.

We take off, going the same direction as the other day. When we turn the corner, Molly stops and unzips her backpack, pulling out the pile of folded papers. She walks up to a somewhat battered silver mailbox by the sidewalk, then pauses and looks at Tanya.

Tanya yanks open the mailbox lid. "I'll open them, you stuff them in. It'll go faster that way."

So Molly stuffs one of the folded papers in the box, Tanya closes it, and we move to the next one. Pretty soon, the girls are jogging from mailbox to mailbox. Open, shove, close. And giggle. They're having so much fun that I'm tempted to join in with a few barks. Instead, I take the chance to pee in a few choice spots.

"We'll be done in no time," Molly says, when we get to the end of the block, and turn to come back down the other side. "We should have made enough for the other streets."

Maybe because they're having so much fun, they don't notice the mail truck that pulls over, parking on the corner where they started. A uniformed mail carrier gets out, carrying a bag over her shoulder. She stops and stares at the girls in a way that makes me nervous. I stare back at her.

Then, she sudden starts towards us, almost running. "Stop!" The way she says it almost sounds like a bark and I answer with one of my own.

Molly and Tanya turn in surprise.

The woman strides up to them. She looks like a shorter, younger version of Mrs. Franklin, dark-skinned with close-cropped curly hair as black as my own. The buttons on her shirt bulge a little, and she has sturdy legs coming down from her shorts. She's wearing fat-soled black shoes that smell faintly of dog poop. Interesting. I thrust my nose closer to investigate.

"Did you know it's a federal crime to put anything in a mail box that isn't stamped U.S. mail?"

Molly and Tanya's eyes widen in surprise. "A crime?" Molly ventures, her voice a little shaky.

"Absolutely. A federal crime."

"But I live here," Tanya insists, a little defiantly. "In the next block." She points. "We're just handing out flyers. No one will mind. They all know my parents."

"The U.S. Post Office minds," the woman says." "You want me telling your mama you got a big fine for breaking the law?"

Tanya shakes her head, blinking hard. Molly's face has gone pale. I pull closer to get a better sniff of the carrier's shoes. Dog poop to be sure, but I don't think it's her dog. She smells like cat. Like several cats, in fact.

"Doodle, no!" Molly says, jerking the harness. Then, apologetically to the woman, "He's friendly."

"I can see that," she says. "Can't work long at this if you can't tell the friendly ones from the ones wanting to take a chunk out of your leg." She bends down and pets me. "But he's sure big. And curly. A poodle?"

"Labradoodle," Molly says, releasing the twisted strand of hair."

"He's a bed-bug dog," Tanya says.

"He finds them for my dad," Molly adds.

The woman grimaces. "Had those once in a place I rented. And my no-good landlord just gave me a can of RAID." Her lips tighten. "I blessed the day I left that sorry place."

"That's awful," Tanya says. "What'd you'd do?"

"Moved out fast as I could. Washed every piece of clothing I own, sprayed every stick of furniture. Put cups under my couch and chairs in case some of 'em moved with me. But I never had them since." She shakes her head. "Don't *ever* want to do that again. I was tempted to take a jar of the vermin and drop 'em off at that slumlord's place. So he could share the experience of having those suckers bite the heck out of him."

The woman pats me a few times and then looks at the paper in Molly's hand. "What you got there?" Wordlessly, Molly hands her a flyer. The woman unfolds it, stares at it a second and then lowers it, her eyes softening. "That Miz Carter's dog who's gone missing? The one that's blind?" She nods in the direction of Mrs. Carter's home. "Lives over there?"

Tanya nods eagerly. "Yeah. He went missing last Tuesday."

"So we're putting out flyers to see if anyone knows what happened when Dan disappeared," Molly adds, her hand twisting a strand of hair.

"Well you can't use mailboxes to do it," the woman says, but her voice has lost all its harshness. She studies the flyer for a moment, then gives it back to Molly. "That woman sure loved that dog. She'd have him with her when she'd come to give me mail. Would watch for me and come out to meet me, 'cause she didn't like to leave outgoing mail in the box. 'Fraid it'd get stolen."

"We think *he* was stolen," Molly says. "That's why we're trying to find out if anyone saw a van in the area."

"A HEAR van," Tanya adds. "We think they've been stealing animals from Black and Latino neighborhoods."

The woman sighs, eyes narrowed, not speaking for a moment. "Last Tuesday?"

"Yeah," Molly and Tanya at the same time.

"There was a HEAR van then. I noticed it, because it was parked right where my mail van is—" she points behind her to the van up the street "—and I didn't like it taking my spot." She smiles. "You know, we get a routine."

"Did you see anyone on Carter's porch?" Molly asks.

The mail woman shakes her head. "No. Two people were getting in, and they pulled away right after. So I got my spot after all. Only time I've seen 'em."

"And you're sure it was Tuesday?" Tanya tells her about Mrs. Carter finding the dog gone but the porch gate latched.

"I'm sure. I have twice the mail to deliver because it's the day the ads come out." She sighs. "Makes me mad to think they might have taken that poor dog. He was the only thing that kept Mrs. Carter together after her husband died. She told me that herself."

"That's why we're trying to find him," Tanya says passionately. "She needs that dog."

Molly asks, "Would you be willing to tell that to Madison Greene? She runs the *Low Down News*."

"Oh. Sorry." The woman shakes her head. "Can't get involved in that kind of stuff. Could get me fired and there's a long line of people eager to take my place." She gives them a sympathetic look. "Sorry." And then, she looks at her watch. "Better get back to work. Or I'll get written up for being too slow."

"What do we do about the flyers? Take them out?"

"What flyers?" the woman asks, winking broadly. "I only saw you put one in this box—" she opens the box and pulls it out, handing it to Tanya "—That's all I know about. But don't do any more."

"So how we gonna get these out?" Tanya ask in a frustrated voice.

The mailwoman thinks a moment. "Well, if you think folks here won't mind, you could maybe put them on the porch. If they do mind, it's trespassing mind you, but that's not my area of concern."

"They won't mind," Tanya says. Molly doesn't look as confident.

The mailwoman adjusts the strap of the bag hanging on her shoulder. "Sure hope you can find that dog."

"Can you keep an eye out for him? In case he just wandered off or something?"

The woman gives them a big smile. "Now that I can do." She turns, walking briskly to the corner and starts putting mail in the boxes.

Molly and Tanya watch her for a bit and then turn to stare at the porch of the house we're in front of.

"I hate going up there," Molly says. "What if someone sees us and gets mad?"

"We could ring the doorbell. If they come to the door, we'll hand it to them."

Molly looks uncertain. "Like those missionaries? Or Jehovah's Witnesses?"

"We won't be preaching at them, just asking about a lost dog. No one will mind that."

"Okay. Here goes nothing. Come on, Doodle."

We all walk up a set of worn and scarred wooden steps to the door of the nearest home. Tanya rings a bell. No answer. She pulls open the screen enough for Molly to stick a flyer in between it and the door jamb.

"See?" Tanya says as we all run down the steps. "That was easy."

But on the next house, I hear slow, shuffling footsteps after the doorbell is rung, and then the door is opened. A very thin, very old man, with a strong medicinal smell mixed with pipe tobacco, peers out at us. He has mottled skin and he's leaning on a walker, bent over in a way that suggests he's not able to straighten up any more. He stares out at us with watery eyes.

Tanya says quickly, "We're looking for Mrs. Carter's lost dog. Do you know Mrs. Carter? She lives across the street."

"Dog?" the man asks, confused. "I don't have a dog."

"No," Molly says, "we're *looking* for a dog that got lost. Mrs. Carter's—"

The man shakes his head carefully in a stiff-necked way. "Don't have a dog."

Tanya says, "No, we're trying to find—" she stops, sighs, and hands him the flyer. "Here," she says. "Have a nice day!"

She turns and starts down the porch, Molly and I following.

"I hope he doesn't live alone," Molly says as we get to the sidewalk.

"What's his name?" Tanya goes to the mailbox. "R. Nelson," she reads. "I'll ask Mama. He might need some help from her church group."

Only one other person answers the doorbell, a friendly young woman with dark circles under her eyes holding a baby in her arms. A toddler peeks out from behind her legs. A dachshund yaps in the background. She listens with sympathy as Tanya tells her—in a raised voice to get over the dachshund's hysterical barking—about Dan.

"Yeah, I heard he was missing," she says, shaking her head. "Poor Mrs. Carter. That dog's all she had to live for. But I was gone most of the day—it's payday and I was grocery shopping."

Molly hands her a flyer anyway. "This has our phone numbers and email. Just in case you hear something from someone or see the HEAR van hanging around."

"Good." The woman shifts the baby in her arms and turns to the dog behind her. "Vixen, hush!"

Vixen doesn't hush.

The woman shakes her head, but doesn't really seem upset. Not sure why, since Vixen's barking is plenty annoying.

"I'll keep my eyes open."

"Thanks so much," Tanya gushes, and then we all turn and head back to the Franklin's house.

We're just turning the corner onto Tanya's street when Molly's phone starts its music.

"Hey, Grady," she says. Without giving him time to respond, she says, "Guess what? We put flyers out in the neighborhoods where Dan disappeared, in case some people saw a HEAR van that day."

"Dan?" Grady sounds confused.

"The blind Jack Russell. If anyone saw anything, they can contact us."

"Oh, yeah. Good." He clears his throat. "Could you come over for a few hours Sunday afternoon and help me train Snippet for the disc throw? Mama said she'd be home all day."

"Should be okay. I'll ask Dad. Sometimes we go to church in the mornings. In the afternoon, Dad usually watches TV and naps."

"I need someone to do the timer," Grady says. "And you can bring Doodle."

Molly promises to text him after she asks her dad.

"I sure hope these flyers work," Tanya says after Molly pockets her phone.

Molly agrees, and, unusually for them, neither say another word until we get back to the Franklins.

Chapter 12

Proof!

A FEW DAYS LATER, MOLLY COMES HOME WITH A plastic box that smells, strangely, of metal, wood, and oil. She sets the case on her bed. I understand the scents when she opens it. Narrow tubes made of dark wood with metal-lined holes are nestled in a soft fabric.

"Isn't it beautiful?" she asks in a hushed tone. "My new oboe." It doesn't look or smell all that great to me, but Molly clearly loves it. "I'm going to learn to play it at school."

Oh. It's an instrument, like the ones the people played in the orchestra for the Christmas pageant that Molly and I were in. I had to be a sheep, and let me tell you, it didn't work out so well. I really don't know much about instruments except the guitar, because that's what the boss plays. Always liked the sound of the guitar. Kind of soothing.

Molly props a skinny book in front of her computer monitor. "My music," she says. "Got to practice."

She takes the tubes out of the case, pushes them together somehow, lifts the thinner end to her mouth, puffs out her cheeks, and blows. Ack! A screech like a cat in excruciating pain bellows from the thing. Fortunately, Molly's door is open. I jump up and escape into the kitchen, as far from the sound as I can get.

Molly continues to make the horrible screeching sounds, until the boss gets up and closes the door to her bedroom. Evidently he can't stand the noise either. Give me a guitar any day.

Finally, after what seems to be a long time, Molly opens her door, and goes to the kitchen. She's grabbing an apple from the fridge when the boss comes in. "How'd it go?" he asks, a silly question since we both know exactly how it went.

"Um, okay." Molly shrugs, looking discouraged. "I'm having trouble getting a good tone."

Duh!

The boss, however, nods in a serious way. "Does your music teacher give lessons? Or know someone who does?"

Molly's face brightens. "Yeah. I think she teaches all the wood-winds. I could ask."

"See what she'd charge," the boss says. "Better to get a good start."

Soon Molly is cutting up vegetables for a salad, while the boss boils water for noodles. Mac and cheese tonight, which hold more promise for scraps than the chicken cream dish. And, in fact, I end up getting a few big bites of Molly's leftovers.

Her phone buzzes just as Molly is loading her plate into the dishwasher. Tanya. Her voice, high with excitement comes over the line.

"Guess what?" She doesn't wait for an answer. "Two people called and said they saw a HEAR van in the neighborhood on Tuesday. And another lady called and said she was telling her next-door neighbor Mr. Williams about the flyers, and he said he saw the van and two people carrying a dog."

"Really?" Molly's eye widen. "He actually saw it?"

"Well, that's what this lady, Mrs. Lewis, said. But she didn't know anything more. Except that now this Mr. Williams wonders what they were doing because his neighbor two houses down—Mama doesn't know those people either—is missing her cat."

"But he saw them take Dan?"

"Mrs. Lewis said he did. Which means we have proof!" Tanya practically shouts the last word.

"Proof!" Molly repeats, in a voice loud enough that the boss sticks his head into the kitchen. "Everything okay?" he asks.

Molly, flustered, nods. "Yeah. Fine. Just talking to Tanya." She waits until he goes back to the living room and turns on the TV before going to her room and shutting the door. I squeeze in, as usual. "You need to call Madison and let her know. She can do an interview and maybe the HEAR people will admit they have Dan."

"Me call her?" Tanya sounds unhappy. "You know her better. I don't think she'd listen to me."

"But you're the one who talked to Mrs. Lewis." For a moment, neither of them speak. Then, Molly sighs and says, "Okay, I'll call Grady." She asks again for the man's name and phone number, writing it down.

But when she tries to call Grady, she gets his voice saying "Not here. Try later."

"I got news," she says into the phone. She taps a key and then does that thing with her thumbs that means she's texting.

"Should I call Madison?" she asks, staring at her phone screen. No clue here. She gives another big sigh and taps her phone, and now Madison's voice is saying, "You have reached Madison Greene of *The Low Down News* . . ."

Molly hesitates, then says, "Hey, it's Molly. I have something you might be interested in. Proof the HEAR people stole Dan."

Before she can put her phone down, it begins to vibrate and play.

"Good," she breathes, pulling it to her ear. "Madison?" A pause. A voice comes over the phone that is definitely not Madison's.

"Oh. Hi, Mom." Molly's face lights up.

"You talk to Madison all the time?" Cori asks, not sounding pleased.

Molly bites her lip. "No, just, um, we're—Tanya and me—are trying to get her help with a missing dog."

"I saw her video blog. When I called to ask her where she got the photos, she told me they came from you."

Molly flushes. "Yeah. She asked me if I had taken any. Sometimes, she pays me for photos."

"And you didn't think to tell me about them? When I'm investigating the incident?"

Molly's face turns even darker. "I didn't think you'd be interested," she says in a low voice.

"Why wouldn't I be interested in photos taken at crime scene?"

Molly looks like a dog caught nosing through the trash.

Cori sighs, and says in a softer tone, "I'm sorry. It's just . . . we're getting nowhere with this, and the bosses are all over us because they responded like it was a terrorist attack and then it turned out to be just some dog thing."

Just some dog thing? What does she mean by that?

"Except, it's not just a dog thing according to the Kensingtons, who think anything that happens to their kid has national importance. And they evidently have some kind of clout. So the brass wants it solved yesterday."

Not sure I follow. I'm not always clear on time, but . . .

"I'm sorry," Molly says, twisting her hair now.

Another sigh from Cori. "Did Madison use all the photos you took? Or are there more?"

"Lots more. I could email all of them. So you can see them." Molly sounds eager now, and turns towards her computer. "I can do it right now."

Cori tells her that would be nice, and then they talk about Armando's visit. By the time Molly says goodbye, she's no longer twisting her hair. She works at her computer for a bit, then says, "Done!" and stands and stretches.

Then she opens the oboe case on her desk, and starts assembling the pieces.

Which is my cue, if ever there was one. I jump up, nose to the door, hoping Molly will get the idea, which fortunately she does. As she turns the handle on the door, she says, "Doodle, I don't think you like the oboe."

Truer words were never spoken.

Chapter 13

Eyewitness

I'M NOT BIG ON DAYS OF THE WEEK LIKE HUMANS ARE, but I do know that whenever it happens to be Saturday, Molly doesn't have to go to school. Plus the boss and I don't usually have to go to work. And if we do, he grumbles about having to work on weekends.

And it turns out tomorrow is Saturday, which means today Molly gets to go to Tanya's. And since I'm *always* invited to go to the Franklin's, I get to go, too. And we're spending the night, because the boss will be at Miguel's, helping him and Annie rebuild his barn,

So, it's a great day, although Molly does her best to spoil it by practicing her oboe right after breakfast. As soon as I see her get the instrument out, I put my nose to the door leading to the backyard. The boss, seeing me, chuckles. "Getting out of Dodge, eh?" he says, a mysterious statement. But he lets me out, taking care to hook my collar to the long chain, something he never forgets since the time I went over the fence. I stretch out in the sun. Even out here, I can hear the squawks coming from the oboe, but they don't hurt my ears the way they do when I'm in the house.

I have a short nap and then Molly comes and gets me, and before long we're in the van on our way to the Franklin's.

"I think I'm getting better," Molly says. "Did you hear me play 'Alouette'?"

From my position in the crate, standing up and looking out, I see the side of the boss's mouth twitch slightly. "Yeah. Great job." His voice has the same fake enthusiasm he uses when calling business clients.

Molly doesn't seem to notice. "Ms. Stenson told us when we checked out our instruments that the more we practice, the better we'll get. So I'm going to try to do an hour a day, half hour in the morning and half hour in the evening."

"That's great," he says, not quite convincingly. "Did you ask her about lessons? If she knows someone who teaches?"

"I'll ask her Tuesday. Everyone who got an instrument has to meet in the music room to get on the schedule for summer."

When we get to Tanya's house, the boss comes in with Molly and me for a few minutes to talk to Mrs. Franklin. As soon as he leaves, Tanya tells her mother that she and Molly are going to take me for a walk. "Just in the neighborhood," Tanya adds reassuringly.

"Okay." Mrs. Franklin looks over at Molly. "Any luck with your Internet searches for Mrs. Carter's dog?"

Molly shakes her head, her face glum. "I've checked every shelter in the county and no one has seen a blind Jack Russell."

"Poor Mrs. Carter," Mrs. Franklin says. "You gonna tell her?"

Tanya and Molly exchange a look. "Not . . . yet," Molly says. "Going to try a couple of more things."

Mrs. Franklin sighs. "I wouldn't want to be the one to have to do that. But," she gives the girls a stern glance, "it's wrong to let her keep hoping, you understand?"

Molly and Tanya nod, solemn-faced, and then go to Tanya's room where Molly puts on my no-pull harness.

"I hope Mr. Williams is home," Molly says, when we're out of the house and on the sidewalk. We're headed in the same direction we took last time to go to Mrs. Carter's, so maybe we're going there after all. "If he saw the HEAR people take Dan, then we'll know . . ."

"Know her poor pup ain't never coming home," Tanya finishes. We reach an intersection and Tanya turns. We end up on the same street where we ran into the mail lady, but walk past the houses where they gave out flyers.

"Three twenty-one," Tanya says, and Molly points across the street. "That one."

We march over to the house and up the steps, onto a porch much like Mrs. Carter's, except not screened in. Four white plastic chairs are grouped around a small table that holds an ashtray full of cigarette butts. Never liked the smell of cigarettes myself. The odor clings to all the furniture.

Molly rings the doorbell, which is the kind that sounds like an angry insect buzzing rather than a bell. Silence. Molly presses the button again, and then I hear footsteps approaching the door. A big man both in height and width answers the door. He's wearing slippers, baggy shorts, and a baggy sweatshirt. His ankles are swollen, and the skin on his legs is pale and mottled. Underneath his tobacco scent is a medicinal one. But he gazes down at us with an intelligent and friendly expression.

"Well, good morning. To what do I owe the pleasure of this visit from such pretty ladies?" he asks. Then, with a grin, "Usually the only folks who ring this bell are door-to-door salesmen or missionaries, and y'all don't like either of those. And they don't usually travel with a dog. Girl Scout cookies, maybe?"

"Mr. Williams?" Tanya ask, her voice a little nervous. When he nods, she continues. "I'm sort of a neighbor. I live over on Bottom Street. The next block over and down a bit? Lamar and Barbara Franklin are my parents. And this is Molly and—" she touches a hand to my head "—Doodle."

Mr. Williams shakes his head, his expression still friendly. "Afraid I haven't met your folks," he says to Tanya. And then, "Doodle, you're one *big* poodle. Didn't know they came in that size."

I wag my tail.

"Yeah, Mama said she didn't think she'd met you. Anyway, we're actually here because of another neighbor, Mrs. Carter. Someone stole her dog—"

"A Jack Russell who's blind," Molly adds, interrupting.

"Yeah," Tanya agrees. "A blind Jack Russell named Dan, and Mrs. Carter is real torn up about it, so we put out flyers to see if anyone had seen anything, and Mrs. Lewis said you saw people from a HEAR van taking a dog—" she pauses "—that's Humanitarians for Enlightened Animal Relations."

"We think the HEAR people might have stolen Dan," Molly says. "And we're trying to get evidence . . ."

Mr. Williams nods again. "That's right. I saw a HEAR van, about two weeks ago, on—" he pauses, thinking — "last Tuesday. I remember that it was Tuesday because that's the day the local ads come in the mail and I was watching for the mail woman. I like to get the coupons. Every cent saved helps." He sighs, his gaze turned inward for a second.

Molly and Tanya exchange a glance.

"So you saw the HEAR van?" Molly as, her voice excited. "We're trying—"

"Would you mind if I sat down?" Mr. Williams interrupts, gesturing at the chairs on the porch. "My legs don't like to stand much these days."

"Sure," says Tanya. Mr. Williams limps over to the larger chair and eases down on it with a little groan. "My joints aren't what they used to be," he says.

After another glance between them, Molly and Tanya pull plastic chairs out and sit facing him.

"So you saw the van?" Molly asks.

Mr. Williams nods. "There were these kids in it. A boy and a girl. Not sure how old they were. High school maybe. Or maybe older." He laughs. "Everyone looks young to me these days."

"Anyway, these kids leave the van and walk down the street, slow like, studying the houses and I watch them because maybe they're casing the neighborhood. But I can't imagine why they'd do such a thing in a van that's so easily recognized. They disappear around the block, and I'm out here watching for the mail lady, and after a little bit they come running back, and one of them is carrying a small brown and white dog. They open the back doors to the van.

"I can't see inside the van because it's parked with the front towards me, but I hear barking. They shove the dog into the back, slam the doors, then get in the front and drive away." He shakes his head and taps the glass top of a table with one finger. "So I figure it must be animal control, picking up strays. But I didn't think HEAR worked for the county. Aren't they the ones always doing the TV ads with the sad dogs behind bars?"

Both Tanya and Molly nod.

"And then Miz Lewis tells me that a dog is missing and some kids were trying to find out about it." He gives them a big smile. "I guess that's y'all."

"They stole Dan—that's the dog—off Mrs. Carter's porch," Tanya says, her voice indignant. "And she loved that dog. We're trying to help her get him back."

Mr. Williams frowns. "Hard to believe they'd steal him. Maybe he got loose somehow?"

"He didn't!" Tanya says earnestly. "Mrs. Carter never leaves him without the latch being locked."

Molly leans forward. "Do you know Madison Greene? The *Low Down News* lady?"

"I've seen her blog, sure, like most everyone else round here."

"We think if she told everyone what happened to Dan, maybe we'd be able to find him. Would you talk to her and tell her your story? If she was willing to come out?"

"Don't really want to stirs things up," Mr. Williams's smile fades and he doesn't speak for a few moments. Then he sighs. "I'll guess I'll tell her my story if she wants it. But I only saw them here on this street. I can't say whether they did or did not take the dog from her porch. You understand? I don't want any lawyers coming after me."

"That's all we want. Just tell her your story. So," Molly lifts her cell phone from her pocket, "we're not sure if she'll want to come or not. But if we could get your phone number?"

Mr. Williams recites a number, which Molly and Tanya both put in their phones. They turn to leave, when Molly stops, still holding her phone.

"Can we give you our numbers?" she asks. "In case the HEAR van comes back? Maybe you could call us?"

Mr. Williams looks amused. "Sure," he says. "Just a second." He goes inside and comes back in a few minutes with a pencil and paper, and then carefully writes down each girl's number.

And then they thank him and we're off. Mr. Williams waves to us as we start down the sidewalk, leaning on the rail of his porch and watching us walk down the street.

"We got proof!" Tanya says triumphantly as soon as we've turned the corner.

"Yeah, and not just hearsay. Someone who actually saw the van."

Tanya grins at Molly. "No hearsay for HEAR, that's our motto."

Molly grins back. She raises a hand to Tanya, who slaps it, just like people are always doing on TV. "No hearsay for HEAR!" she repeats emphatically.

They giggle and then break into a jog, and before long we're back at the Franklin's.

Chapter 14

Mr. Blevins

I WONDER HOW MUCH SHE PAID FOR THIS HOUSE," THE boss says, as we pull into Grady's driveway. "Eighteen hundred square feet and a double garage in a nice neighborhood. Bet it's at least three quarters of a million."

Molly unsnaps her seatbelt. "You could ask."

"I could ask to see her bank statements and tax returns, too."

Molly gives him a quizzical look, and with a smile he explains, "It's not polite to ask people what they paid for things, unless you're talking about groceries or sales or such."

"I'm not sure if she'd care, since she's always blogging," Molly says, as she opens the side door to let me out of my crate.

"But about other people's lives, not hers."

The front door opens and Madison sticks her head out.

"Okay, I'm out of here," the boss says. "Got a nap with my name on it waiting at the house and I don't want to get sucked into a long conversation."

Naps can have names?

Molly slams the door shut and moves in front of the van as the boss backs away, giving a little wave to Madison. She waves back, then nods at us as we come into the tiled entryway.

"Snippet's in the backyard," she says. "I thought Doodle could play with her while you two do me a favor."

Grady, comes in from the kitchen, a half-eaten apple in his hand. "Favor?"

Madison gives them both a bright smile. "I was waiting for Molly to be here so I don't have to explain it twice. Grady told me about those flyers you put out for that missing dog —" she gestures at Molly "—and that gave me an idea as to how I might find out more about our *friendly*—" she lifts her eyebrows as she emphasizes the word "—neighbor, Mr. Blevins."

Molly sucks in her breath.

Madison nods. "Our favorite person, right? Before I respond to his lawyer—who, incidentally does *not* have an impressive resume and I suspect will be quickly out of his depth if my lawyers need to contact him—I'd like to know more about Mr. Blevins. I have a suspicion that his "your-dog-bit-me" routine might have played in other venues. I bet there are other people he's bullied into making some kind of settlement. I'm going to investigate where he lived before he moved here."

"When was that?" Grady asks.

"A little over three years ago. And, before that, he lived in Southern California."

Madison pulls back her hair, twists it into a knot on top of her head, then lets it drop. "But I have a problem. I don't know most of my neighbors yet, and probably won't for some time as we don't really go to church and Grady doesn't go to the local school. And I need to know if Blevins has had problems with neighbors here, anything that might not have gone to court so it wouldn't be in the public record. It could be very useful information down the road."

She points at a narrow table in the entryway. "So, borrowing a page from Miss Molly here, I created a flyer of my own—more of a note, really—that I'd like you two to deliver to all the homes in, say, a three-block radius."

Molly is nodding as she goes over to the table and opens one of the flyers. "Oh, you mention the one-bite law," she says approvingly.

"I thought that would be good information for our neighbors to have, given Mr. Blevins's presence in the area. So they can know he's, um, pardon the expression, blowing hot air. And I have a request for anyone who has had problems with a neighbor threating legal action concerning a dog to contact me."

"Can you do that?" Grady asks. "I mean, can he sue us or anything?"

"He's *already* suing us," Madison says dryly. "Or at least threatening to. But, no, I'm not mentioning him by name, although I hope to high heaven he hears about it, the sooner the better. He needs to understand what he's up against. What might have worked before will *not* work here."

"Okay," Molly says eagerly. "We can do that. I'll put Doodle out back." She glances at Grady. "We'll still have time to practice."

So, before long, Snippet and I are watching through the fence slats as Molly and Grady set off down the sidewalk. Snippet barks a few times to let Grady know we'd rather not be left behind, but after they turn into the yard of the house next door, we give up and start a game of chase. It hardly seems like much time at all before we hear their voices approaching the house and Molly and Grady are back.

They join us outside, Grady carrying several bright plastic discs. This could be fun. I love playing keep-away with discs.

But, sadly, Grady hands Molly a stopwatch and she makes me lie down beside her while Grady throws the disc for Snippet. Molly's job, it appears, is to call out the time after every catch. Mine is to do nothing. I would think Snippet might get tired of chasing those discs, since every single time she brings one back to Grady he throws it again. Chase the disc, bring it back. Chase disc, bring it back. What's the point in that? The whole thing could be *much* more interesting if we both chased the disc to see who could grab it first. (I'll tell you who!)

Just when I'm thinking that a nap would be nice, the doorbell rings. Snippet drops the disc and rushes to the gate to bark. Not to be left out, I join her, as do Grady and Molly. A skinny-legged, big-bellied figure wearing a baseball cap is standing in front of the door.

"Blevins!" Grady says, just as I catch a whiff of the man's scent and recognize him. He and Molly exchange a look. "I guess it worked," Grady says. "Unless he's here to add to the lawsuit."

Molly and Grady hurry to the back door. Snippet and I push through into the house along with them.

When we all get to the living room, Mr. Blevins is still standing in the doorway, beads of sweat showing on his forehead under the hat visor. He's wearing shorts like before, bushy leg hair sprouting over his thin legs that go down to the same white thick-soled shoes.

"—assume this is about me?" he is saying as we all click across the tile and cluster behind Madison. He brandishes the flyer like it's a weapon, flapping it at Madison.

Madison runs a hand through her hair. "I don't believe anyone is specifically named," she says, her face a picture of innocence. "And I certainly can't help what you assume." She gives him a brief, cold smile.

"You're trying to ruin my reputation." He flaps the paper again for emphasis.

"To repeat myself," Madison says sweetly, "no one is named in that document. If, however, you feel the shoe fits . . ."

I glance at his feet. As far as I can tell, his shoes fit fine.

Mr. Blevins scowls at her, then presses his lips tightly together. He takes a deep breath and finally says, in a more normal tone, "Look, I don't want to be a bad neighbor. I feel we got off to a bad start."

"You mean with your using our lawn for your dog's potty area?" Madison asks, her voice still sweet but her eyes cold.

Another scowl followed by another deep breath. "I'm . . . I'm sorry about that. I didn't know anyone had moved in. This place was vacant for some time."

Madison doesn't reply, but watches him, waiting.

"Since I wasn't really hurt *badly*—" he rubs the back of his hand "—and I was in your front yard, how about we call a truce? I'll withdraw the suit if you don't pursue this further, either in the neighborhood or legally."

Molly and Grady exchange a triumphant look, but Madison stands stock still and waits a long time before replying. "I believe I can do that," she says at last, "if you will apologize to my son and his fine friend for maligning the reputation of these two *sweet* dogs."

Now it's Mr. Blevins's turn to be silent. He swallows, his lips puckering as if he has a bad taste in his mouth. Finally, he mumbles, "Sorry."

Madison frowns. "I'm not sure they were able to hear—"

But Grady steps forward, interrupting her. "Thank you, sir," he says in a voice more polite than I've ever heard him use. "Snippet." When the dog comes to his side, he says, "Sit." Snippet sits. Then, to Mr. Blevins he says, "I'd like you to meet Snippet. So you'll know she would never hurt anyone. And so she'll know you're a . . ." he hesitates on the word ". . . friend."

After a brief pause, Mr. Blevins tentatively reaches out a hand and pats Snippet on the head. She sits politely, a Canine Good Citizen through and through.

Grady gives Molly a questioning glance, but she shakes her head and shrinks back from the door.

"Thank you, sir," Grady says, still in his abnormally polite voice.

Mr. Blevins nods and then meets Madison's eye. "So, we're good?" he asks.

"Mr. Blevins, I believe we are as fine as a sunny day in Georgia," Madison says, laying on the drawl and extending her hand. Mr. Blevins shakes it, and then turns and walks away.

Madison, watching him go. "I guess that's a slam-dunk! But I sure didn't think he'd find out about the flyers so soon. We must have very gossipy neighbors."

"No," Molly says, beaming at Grady with pride. "He found out about the flyers because Grady marched up to his door, rang the bell, and handed him one!"

Madison turns and stares open-mouthed at her son. "Why Grady Jefferson Greene!" she says, her voice filled with admiration.

Grady runs his fingers through his straight-up hair, clearly pleased. "Well, you said you wanted him to find out. And you said sooner rather than later . . ." He grins up at his mother.

"Well, you certainly were right." Madison shuts the door and says, "I think we've all done our good deed for the day. This calls for a treat. Who wants ice cream?"

Snippet and I don't get ice cream, of course, but Madison surprises me by handing each of us a peanut butter chew, which is fine by us.

In between spoons of what smells like chocolate mint ice cream, Molly tells Madison about how the flyers she and Tanya put out resulted in finding out about Mr. Williams, and how he saw the HEAR van.

"So now we have proof," she says, eagerly.

Madison shakes her head impatiently, then sighs. She says, her voice sympathetic, "It's not really proof. One man's word against a big organization with lots of lawyers on board. What we'd need—what I'd need, anyway—is hard evidence. Photos, video footage, something that physically connects them to the neighborhood on that day." She touches Molly's arm. "Sorry."

Molly, clearly disappointed, stirs her ice cream. "Okay."

Grady frowns at his mother, and for a while everyone eats in silence. Then Molly's phone buzzes. "Dad's here," she says after checking it. "Gotta go."

Madison jumps up. "Why don't you invite him in?" She gives Molly a bright smile. "We have plenty more ice cream."

"We, um, that is, we can't," Molly says apologetically. "But thanks for everything." She clips on my leash and hurries through the door before Madison can say anything else.

Chapter 15

Caught in the Act

MOLLY HAS JUST FINISHED GIVING ME THE CRUST from her after-school peanut butter sandwich when her phone bursts into music. She glances at it, smiles and taps the screen.

"The HEAR van is back!" Tanya's practically shouting with excitement. "Mr. Williams saw it drive by slowly, and then park on the other side of the street on the corner!"

Molly absorbs this information for a second. "If I could get photos—"

"Then we'd have what Madison wants," Tanya says. "Can you come over? Mama won't be home from work for another half hour. Could your dad bring you? We could practice our Spanish dialogue, so you could say it's homework."

"Oh, yeah. I forgot about that. Let me check." Molly hurries into the boss's bedroom, where he's at his desk doing paperwork, something he hates almost as much as traffic.

"I forgot I need to go to Tanya's," she says.

The boss's brow creases. "Why?"

"We have a Spanish dialogue due on Friday and we were going to practice it tomorrow. But I forgot I'm going to Mom's tomorrow for class night instead of her house. And Tanya has some church thing on Thursday."

Forgot? We usually get fast food on class night (by "we" I mean the boss and Molly, as it's always kibble for me) and then the boss drops us at Tanya's. But Cori called the boss a few days ago and invited Molly to come to dinner while Armando is in town.

"And she even invited Doodle," the boss said, when he gave Molly the news. Since then, Molly has talked of little else. So it surprises me that she forgot.

Maybe it surprises the boss, too, because the lines on his forehead deepen.

"Please?" Molly asks, with what I call her dog-begging-for-food face. "Could you take me over? Just for a couple of hours? We'll do our dialogue and then we can take Doodle for a short walk."

The boss sighs and grumbles about being a live-in taxi service, but he gets up from his desk and pulls out his keys. "You'll need his harness then. And a jacket. There's a chilly breeze. And it might rain."

"I know," Molly says. She shrugs into her windbreaker and fits my no-pull harness around me and we head out to the van. Before long, we're making the turn into Tanya's driveway.

Tanya meets us at the door, already wearing the hoodie she uses for a jacket, and as soon as the boss's van is out of sight, she says, "Let's go. I hope we're not too late!"

Molly snaps the leash on my harness, but just as we start out, Mrs. Franklin pulls into the driveway.

"Where're you going?" she asks. She eases herself out of the van and walks stiffly toward us, smoothing the skirt of her maid's uniform. She looks tired.

"Taking Doodle for a walk," Tanya says, with an anxious glance down the street.

"And practicing our Spanish dialogue," Molly adds.

"I need you to help me unload these groceries."

Molly and Tanya exchange a look, but then hurry over to carry sacks into the house. When they're done, Mrs. Franklin says, "Since you're walking, why don't you go over to Mrs. Carter's and tell her you can't find Dan."

Neither girl speaks for a moment.

Finally, not meeting her mother's pointed stare, Tanya mumbles, "Okay."

And then, at last, we're off. Tanya and Molly half-walk, half-run down the street, speaking lines of Spanish back and forth as they go. I concentrate on the breeze, more of a wind, actually, which speaks a language of its own through the scents it delivers straight to my nose.

When we get to the end of the block and turn the corner, Tanya gasps and stops dead. "Is that—" she points straight ahead "—their van?"

The only van I see is a white one near the end of the block, parked with its back towards us.

"I can't read the lettering," Molly says, squinting. "And I can't see if anyone is in it." She grabs her camera from her windbreaker and holds it up. "I'll zoom in," she says. And then, "HEAR! It *is* their van!" And then, with amazement, "And one of the back doors is slightly open." She holds the camera up to her eye again. "Someone is in front of the van. A guy. Wait! A guy and girl."

"What if they have dogs in there?" Tanya asks, her voice worried. "That they stole?"

Molly's eyes widen at the thought. "What if . . ." she skews her face in concentration. "Maybe you could walk Doodle to the front and talk to them. And I could look in the van. And get photos. In case anyone is missing a pet."

Now it's Tanya's turn to think. "Okay. I could ask them about Dan. I mean, if they took him, they probably won't admit it, but I could ask." Her eyes light up. "Maybe I could pretend I want to join or something."

Molly nods. "Yeah. That might keep them talking."

They both start walking at a faster pace.

We pass Mrs. Carter's house, with the screened porch. Molly and Tanya are so focused on the van they don't even give it a glance.

As we get closer, I can hear talking over the slapping of the girls' shoes on the sidewalk. Two voices, one male and one female. We walk some more before the girls hear it. They stop again.

"Here we go," Molly says in a low voice. "In front." She hands my leash to Tanya. "Go on ahead. Try to keep them looking away from the van. I'm going to see what's inside the open door. Talk loud in case it creaks."

Tanya nods, swallowing hard. "Come on, Doodle." She takes off at a jog, slowing down when we pull alongside the van.

A man, well, really a teenager, is leaning against the front of the van smoking, talking to a woman who looks a little older. The woman takes a drink from a water bottle. Hey, I recognize her. She's the vegan lady from the dog fair. Same hair badly in need of a groom. Same acned face.

Tanya recognizes her as well. "Oh, hey there," she says brightly. "I know you. Sue . . . Suzie?" Despite the scent of anxiety pouring from her, Tanya gives the girl a big, if somewhat fake-looking smile.

"Suzanne," the girl says severely.

"Suzanne. Yeah. We met at the Arlington DogDays, remember?"

"I remember." Not a pleasant memory, judging by Suzanne's expression.

"I'm Tanya." She smiles again at Suzanne and nods at the boy.

"Jason," he mumbles.

Tanya forges ahead. "So, you work for HEAR," she says in a loud voice. "I've heard lots of things about them. Do you get to, like, save lots of animals and stuff? You must love animals."

Both the Jason and Suzanne stare at Tanya for a second as if she's speaking Chinese—a difficult language most people, and dogs for that matter, don't understand. Then Jason recovers. He stubs out his cigarette against the van.

"Yeah," he says. "Love animals and protect them. We help the creatures on this planet who have no one to stick up for them."

There's something about his scent that's familiar. I sniff harder, trying to place it. Oops. Maybe I got a little too close.

"Hey, get him off of me!" he says, in a voice that is not at all loving. He shoves my head away from his leg.

"Oh, sorry." Tanya pulls on the leash unnecessarily since I'm already back at her side. I can feel her hand trembling through the leather. "Do you, um, have to be a certain age to join?"

Suzanne scowls, looking down at me. "Isn't that your friend's dog? That long-haired girl?"

"Molly?" Tanya says brightly, still in a louder than usual voice. "Yeah. She's my best friend and sometimes I watch her dog for her, and like, take him for walks, and things."

Underneath her voice, as she rattles on, I hear a soft squeak, like a door being opened.

Suzanne says, her voice contemptuous, "Well, you should tell your friend that dog breeders are no better than Nazis with their eugenics. Trying to get the perfect conformation to a breed while millions of dogs suffer. Their kennels are nothing more than concentration camps for dogs. Meanwhile, millions of dogs die in shelters every day who aren't adopted because breeders flood the market with their dogs. And designer dogs are the worst." She glares at Tanya the way a dog might at someone threatening to steal its food.

"Except they don't starve. Dogs in kennels." Tanya says, her voice now stringy with tension. "At least, in good kennels."

Suzanne brushes an oily lock of hair from her face. "There are no good ones. And they absolutely do starve in many kennels and live in appalling conditions. Haven't you heard of puppy mills?"

"Yeah, but . . ." She swallows and takes a deep breath, regrouping. She gives Suzanne and Jason another fake smile. "Hey, have either of you seen a Jack Russell? Older dog. And he's blind. He went missing last week from a friend's house right on this street." Her voice is bright and cheerful again. She turns and starts to point toward the back of the van, then jerks her arm back, whirls back to point down the street in front of the van.

Another glance between Suzanne and Jason. I'm still trying to place his scent. So familiar, yet elusive.

"Don't remember any Jack Russells," Jason says, his face turning red and now, his voice suddenly pinched.

"You sure?" Tanya squares her shoulders, and her tone changes from friendly to accusing. "'Cause one of the neighbors saw your van on the same day that Dan—that's the dog—disappeared."

"Couldn't have seen it. We were one block over!" Jason blurts, earning him a scathing look from Suzanne.

"We rescue too many dogs to—" Suzanne stops as a clunking sound, like something metallic falling can be heard. "What was that?" She turns to stare at the back of the van.

"Are you sure about Dan?" Tanya asks, her voice even louder. But her face is screwed in dismay, and she darts a glance behind her.

I follow her gaze and see a brief flash of light—like lightning but weaker. Molly's camera flash, I realize.

Suzanne fixes Tanya with a suspicious glare. "What's going on?"

"What the—?" Jason says. He springs away from the van and lunges at Tanya, but she leaps out of reach, shouting, "Molly, *run!*"

Tanya takes off, me at her side. When we get to Molly, she's bent into the doorway of the van, her camera flashing.

"Come *on*," Tanya says, grabbing her arm.

Molly backs out, and starts to run, but then she trips, sprawling on the ground. Her camera flies out of her hand, clattering on the pavement ahead of us.

"Ow," she cries out in pain. Tanya swoops up the camera, and then grabs Molly's hand just as Jason comes running up to us.

"Stop!" he shouts. "Give me that camera. Give it to me right now or I'll—"

I don't like his tone. I don't like his tone or the way he's shouting at the girls, like a Rottweiler bullying a small dog. The leash yanks my collar as Tanya, Molly now beside her, starts to run down the road, but I stand firm and it pulls free from her hand.

Suzanne yells, "Stop! We'll have you arrested!"

But the girls keep going, their shoes smacking as they hit the pavement.

I stare at Jason and growl.

Jason stops dead, his face filled with apprehension.

"We got a vicious one here," he says, with an agonized glance at the fleeing girls. "Get the dog pole."

Suzanne says, "Right!" She reaches into the van.

I stand my ground, growling.

Ahead, almost to the corner, Molly stops and whirls around. "Doodle!" she calls, her voice harsh with fear. "*No bite!* Doodle, come! *Come!*" I look at her, and then at Suzanne, who is coming toward me with a long pole.

"*Doodle!*" Molly cries out again. I've never heard her sound more scared. She needs me. I turn and bound away, racing to her.

"Oh, Doodle," she says, relief flooding her voice as she grabs my leash. And then we're all running again until, at the end of the street, Molly slows and glances over her shoulder. I turn to look as well.

Neither Suzanne nor Jason are chasing us. They both stand beside the back doors of the van.

Molly pulls out her camera and clicks it a few times.

Then Suzanne raises something and points it towards us.

"She's got a camera," Molly shouts, grabbing Tanya by the shoulder and turning her away from the van. "Don't let them get our faces!" We scramble around the corner, racing down the street until we get to Tanya's house.

"Here," Tanya says, opening the side gate to the back yard. They burst through the gate and plop to the ground, breathing hard, sweaty and flushed-faced. Come to think of it, despite the chilly breeze, I'm panting as well.

"Keep down," Tanya says. They shed their jackets and crawl over to the fence to peer through the slats. Hey, I'm good at this, having spent much of my life behind fences. I stand beside them, where I can see the road.

A white van drives by slowly.

"There it is!" Molly says in a fierce whisper.

We all watch as it passes and turns at the end of the street. Neither Molly nor Tanya move when it's gone, but watch for quite a bit longer. Finally Tanya says, "I don't think they're coming back."

The girls stand up. Molly picks up her jacket and puts it back on, shivering a little. No trace of sunlight now in the dark gray sky.

"My camera," Molly says, her face lined with worry. "I hope it isn't broken." She touches Tanya's arm. "Thanks for getting it. I waited too long."

"No kidding," Tanya says fervently. "I thought we might *all* end up in that van."

At that, Molly shudders. "Doodle," she says, throwing her arms around my neck. "What if they'd got you?"

Got me? Wasn't going to happen. But I lick her fingers because she's so upset. They're very salty.

I take a long drink from the bowl of water Mrs. Franklin keeps for me by the back door.

Tanya digs Molly's camera from her coat pocket and hands it to her. "So, did you get anything? Were there any dogs inside?"

"No dogs. Or cats. But I got photos of the inside of the van. They had cages, and—" her brow creases as she pushes buttons on her camera. "Looks—"

But at that moment, the backdoor creaks open and Mrs. Franklin stands behind the screen.

"I thought I heard voices," she says. "How'd it go with Mrs. Carter?"

Chapter 16

Awkward Conversations

Y OU DIDN'T TALK TO HER." MRS. FRANKLIN SAYS, READ-
ing the dismay on the girls' faces.

"No," Tanya says, in a low voice.

"But we had a reason," Molly adds.

"You'd better come in and tell me about it. Too cold out here." Without another word, Mrs. Franklin disappears. We follow her into the house.

"We saw the HEAR van—the one that took Dan." Tanya takes a deep breath, and then tells her mother how she talked to the drivers while Molly took photos. She doesn't tell her about being chased by the drivers. Not sure why.

Mrs. Franklin is silent for a long time after she finishes. With her hands on her broad hips, she stares at the girls with a stern look that has each of them fidgeting. At last, she shakes her head. "I hope none of that was illegal—getting into the van and all that."

"The door was open," Molly says in a low voice. "I didn't go in, just stood outside and shot the photos."

"Well that's something. At least you weren't breaking and entering." She grimaces. "I hope you both remember," she says softly, "that sometimes the law can be a lot harder on blacks than whites. Black boys have been shot on the street for less than what you two did. *No* dog is worth that."

Molly and Tanya both nod. Molly's head is down, her eyes on the floor.

Mrs. Franklin sighs. "But I guess technically you didn't break any laws." She sighs again.

"And we found real evidence," Tanya says after a bit. "So maybe Madison can stop them from stealing dogs from people like Mrs. Carter."

"Speaking of Mrs. Carter . . ." Mrs. Franklin looks from one girl to the other.

Molly and Tanya exchange another glance. Then, Molly says, "I'll call her. I'm the one who suggested helping her search. It was my idea."

"You sure?" Tanya asks.

Molly nods, her face pale but resolute. She asks Mrs. Franklin for the number and taps it into her phone. I hear that soft grating sound it always makes before people answer.

"Hello?" comes a hesitant voice from the speaker.

"Mrs. Carter?" Molly's voice is tight and unusually high. "This is Molly Hunter. Tanya's friend? I don't know if you remember me."

"Oh, yes," Mrs. Carter says, her voice warm now. "I remember you well. You helped bring the cake. How are you doing?"

Mrs. Franklin and Tanya are both staring at Molly with intense interest. It's hard to tell how much they hear, being human and lacking the keen senses that dogs have.

Molly scrunches up her eyes. "Fine, but we were calling, that is, I am calling—"

"Did you find anything about Dan?" Mrs. Carter interrupts, her voice eager.

There is a short pause before Molly answers. "I'm sorry. We didn't. We checked every place we could think of, but . . ." her voice trails off.

For a moment, Mrs. Carter doesn't speak. "Well, I appreciate you trying. It was very nice of you. I just miss him so—" she goes silent for a moment. Then, she thanks Molly several more times. "For making the effort," she says. "Thank Tanya, too. Her family has always been good to me. Miz Franklin, she's one of the best."

Molly says goodbye and pockets her phone.

"She said to thank you, too," Molly tells Tanya. Then, to Mrs. Franklin, "She says to tell you you're 'one of the best.'"

"Well, don't know about that." Mrs. Franklin shakes her head slowly. After another long silence, she says, "Well, you two have had quite a day. Don't know what I think about it, but I'm glad you told me. Now get on and let me mull this over." She makes a shooing motion with her hands.

The girls don't need to be told twice. As soon as we're in Tanya's bedroom with the door shut and locked, Molly takes out her camera, fiddles with it, snaps a few photos, and then sighs with relief. "It's okay," she says, sinking down on Tanya's bed. "It still takes pictures. And all the photos seem to be there."

"Let me see," Tanya says. She climbs up beside Molly. I can't see anything, of course, so I settle down on the floor.

"Needles," Tanya says at one point. "And look at all those bottles. What does it say?"

They both stare intently at the camera's little screen. "Phenobarbital," Tanya says after a bit.

"Look at this!" Molly sounds excited.

"Too small to read," Tanya says. "Make it bigger." And then, "They're . . . schedules."

"Of all the dog events in the area," Molly says triumphantly. "And now this one."

"Paint bombs?" Tanya asks.

"Blue and yellow, just like at the dog fair!" Molly holds her hand up in the air and Tanya slaps it, like I sometimes see athletes do on T.V.

They mull over the photos for a while longer, then Molly puts the camera back in her pocket. "Will you be in a lot of trouble?" she asks.

"I don't think so, or Mama would have already said. But I *had* to tell her. You could see she just *knew* something was up. She always does. And if she found out from a neighbor that someone saw us there?" Tanya rolls her eyes. "I'd be on restriction until I got out of college." Tanya falls silent for a second. "She'll tell your dad."

Molly nods. "I think he'll be okay. Probably just give me a lecture." And then, she sits up straight. "I gotta call Madison. We now have *physical* proof!" She pulls out her phone, but stops and doesn't tap it. "Maybe I should call Mom, first. Now that we have evidence."

"She could arrest them," Tanya agrees with enthusiasm.

"But . . ." Molly thinks about it. "She might be mad that we were there." She frowns.

"She'll probably find out anyway," Tanya says. "Since Mama will tell your dad."

"Yeah." Molly swallows, and taps the phone a couple of times.

"Hey, Mom," she says, when Cori answers. "Guess what?"

Molly launches into a long account about the HEAR van, which isn't news to me—been there, just did that a little while ago—so I take the opportunity to nap. She's still on the phone when Mrs. Franklin knocks on the door and announces the boss has come to pick us up.

"Gotta go," Molly says, trying to shrug into her windbreaker one-handed. "I'll send you everything from home."

The boss, standing just behind Mrs. Franklin, gives Molly a curious glance. "Was that your mother?"

When Molly nods, he asks, "Send her what?"

"I'll tell you on the way home," Molly says.

Mrs. Franklin says, "Just be sure to tell him *everything*." She gives the boss a pointed look. "They insist they've done nothing illegal."

Molly flushes.

"Let's go then," the boss says in a tight voice. He thanks Mrs. Franklin and soon we're climbing into the van.

"Well?" the boss asks, his head bent over his shoulder as he backs out of the driveway. "What was Mrs. Franklin talking about?" His fingers begin rapping on the steering wheel.

Molly starts into the story yet again, her voice shaky at first, but then gaining strength. I resume my nap.

I wake up to the van slowing down and easing into our driveway.

"—I told her I'd send her all my photos. And that's it." Molly takes a deep breath, eyeing the boss nervously.

He gets out of the car without a word, and walks stiff-shouldered to the door in silence. Only after he's unlocked it and we've gone into the deliciously spaghetti-scented house, does he speak. "Did you get any Spanish done at all?" he asks. "Or was that just something you made up?"

Whoa. No mistaking the anger in his voice.

"I didn't make it up. We practiced on the way to Mrs. Carter's," Molly says. And then, with a sharp intake of breath, her eyes on the boss's face, "But, I guess . . ." She lets the breath out. "It was kind of an excuse." She's silent for a moment. "But now maybe Mom can arrest them."

The boss shakes his head. "You can't save the world, Molly. And Mrs. Franklin was right. You and Tanya could have been in danger. I don't want you taking chances like that."

Molly nods without speaking. And, in fact, neither the boss nor Molly talk much during dinner. But by bedtime, after much time on her computer and several phone calls to her mom, Molly is much more cheerful.

"I'm glad I called her," she tells me as I curl down on the rug by her bed. "She's going to check it out. And she's okay if I send some of the photos to Madison."

Not sure why any of that is important, but if Molly says it is, it must be.

Chapter 17

Meeting the Family

Tonight's the night the boss has his classes. After Christmas, he told Molly that he wanted to go back to school because he thought a degree would help him get more customers, something he's always worrying about. "A degree will look better in our ads," he said. "So they know I'm not just some random guy with a dog and a business license." The boss has said this last part many times before. He's always worrying about it. "And most of my credits from Surry Community College will transfer. I'm only ten short for an associate's degree."

No idea what he means about credits, but now he goes to school one night a week and takes two classes, business management and English. I'm a little surprised about English because he already speaks it very well. I mean, no one has trouble understanding him, which is not the case when, say, he tries to talk in Spanish.

Molly has to change clothes several times before settling on what she wants to wear—this happens a lot when she's going to see her mother—and then we're off, because the boss wants to leave early enough to avoid traffic.

Cori's house doesn't have a driveway, and the boss has to go up half a block beyond it before he finds parking. We walk past several small houses with narrow yards that look much like Cori's, although, of course, they each have a distinct scent.

"New sidewalk?" the boss asks, as we turn into her yard and head for the door.

"Yeah, she had it done last fall," Molly says.

Come to think of it, last time I was here, the sidewalk was cracked and weedy. Smelled about the same, though, with the scent of Miga, Cori's cat, everywhere.

"And new flower beds." Molly points to two strips of dirt in front of the house dotted with small green plants. Then she hurries ahead and presses the doorbell. Before the buzzer stops, the door is flung open and a swell of voices and laughter pours out from inside. But I'm more interested in the scents that come with the sound: meat, cheese, tortillas, people, and, of course, Miga.

"It's not Silvia," Armando shouts over his shoulder, "it's our María Molly." He smiles at Molly. "We thought it might be our daughter, but you're just as good." He opens his arms to embrace Molly. He doesn't smell as strongly of Mexican food as when we saw him in his restaurant, but he's dressed the same, in dark jeans, black shirt, and brightly colored vest.

Molly hugs him, her face lit up with happiness, something that always seems to happen when she's with Armando.

"Have fun," the boss says, handing her my leash. He turns to go.

But Armando calls out, "Josh! Good to see you!" and steps out to give him a hug as well, patting him vigorously on the back like some people pat dogs. The boss returns the hug stiffly, but with a smile.

And then Mariela, calm and dignified, her silvery hair pulled back into a bun, appears in the doorway. "Molly," she says, her voice filled with warmth.

Armando jumps a little as a beep comes from his pocket. "Ah," he says pulling out a phone and glancing at the screen. "Silvia's going to be late."

"No surprise there," Mariela gives Molly an apologetic smile. "Our daughter is late more often than she's on time."

"Josh," she says, giving the boss a friendly nod, and then she turns to Molly, "Come in. We're all so excited to see you."

Molly flushes, her expression at once eager and a little scared. The boss starts down the sidewalk and Molly and I go inside.

Sitting in her recliner, near the back wall of the room, is Benita, Cori's aunt, looking the same as the last time I saw her, dressed in jeans and a flowery patterned blouse, her gray hair pulled back into a bun. Still wearing those thick soled white tennis shoes with wool socks, too.

According to Molly, Benita is Cori's mother's sister. Confusing, right? As I said earlier, dogs keep it simple. Most only know their mother and their brothers and sisters, and only then while they're puppies. But Molly has always been what the boss calls family hungry—because, he says, of Cori's leaving them so long ago—and Molly seems to love all this complicated maternal, paternal, aunt and uncle and cousin stuff.

On Benita's lap, sits a small boy, barefoot, his chubby legs sticking out from baggy shorts. And on his lap is Miga. He clutches the cat tightly to his chest. Miga does not look happy, her ears flattened against her head. If I were that little boy, I'd worry about getting scratched.

"María," Benita calls across the room to Molly.

Mariela touches Molly on the shoulder, and inclines her head toward Benita, and says in a low voice, "I'm happy to see your great aunt looking so well. Before this trip, I hadn't seen her, in—" she shakes her head "—I don't know how many years. I think it's wonderful that she was able to take Cori in, back when—" her hand tightens on Molly's shoulder for a second "—when she left." She sighs and pats Molly's shoulder. "Got to get back to work. I promised your mother I'd do most of the cooking."

Maybe Cori hears this, because she now appears in the doorway to the kitchen. "Hey, Molly," she says, smiling. "We're almost ready to eat. Just have to finish a few things. Mariela's trying to teach me to cook chili rellenos, which might be a lost cause." She turns back into the kitchen, Mariela following her.

Armando leads us across the room to Benita, who pries the boy's arms away from Miga, and slides him off her lap. The cat shoots across the room and down the hall, while Benita rises carefully in that stiff way older people have. She hugs Molly, but pulls away when the boy emits an ear-piercing squeal.

"Oggie!" he shouts. "Oggie!" He launches himself toward me. I sit in surprise. He grabs at an ear, but I back away. "Oggie!" A strong scent of urine wafts from his diaper, and a fainter one of cookies from his face.

"Tony!" shouts Armando. He sweeps the protesting child into his arms, and says, while holding the struggling boy, "Molly, let me introduce my grandson, Tony. He's in his tyrannical twos, I'm afraid."

"Hi," Molly says, but Tony's attention—rather, his rage—is centered on his grandfather. "Down! Down! Oggie!" he screams, his pudgy legs kicking wildly.

Armando holds Tony away from his body, his voice deepening. "Tony, *stop* or I will have to take you to the other room. *Stop* if you want down."

Tony doesn't seem to hear. "Et Oggie! Et Oggie!" he screams.

"I'll take him." Mariela hurries from the kitchen, and reaches for the boy. She holds him in a firm grip. "Stop it *ahorita*! You cannot pet the doggie until you stop." He reduces his cries to a whimper. And then, pulling her hand away from his bottom, she crinkles her nose. "You need a new diaper."

"No! Et Oggie." he howls, back to full volume. She carries him across the room and down the hall. A door shuts and suddenly everything is quieter. Benita sinks back down in her chair and Armando takes a seat on the couch, gesturing for Molly to join him.

"Whew!" Armando sighs. "We're watching Tony for my son Rodrigo and his wife. He just got a job with a big accounting firm in D.C. I wish you could have met them, but they only got the keys to their apartment two days ago and are still living in boxes."

Living in boxes?

"As you can see," Armando says with another sigh, "unpacking will be a lot easier without Tony."

After a bit, Mariela returns, holding a tear-stained but thankfully silent Tony. The strong urine odor is gone, replaced (mostly) by a perfumy lavender scent. She sets him on the floor beside me. "Be gentle. Soft," she commands.

"Oggie," Tony says. He makes me a little nervous and I find myself panting slightly, but this time Tony doesn't grab at my ear and his quick pats on my back, while not exactly *soft,* don't hurt.

The doorbell rings. I bark, startled, and Tony jumps back and grabs Mariela's legs. She swoops him up and settles on the couch. "Oggie loud!" he says, giving me an accusing glare.

Seriously? Look who's talking.

Armando's face lights up. "Silvia!" He hurries to open the door.

A young woman enters, dressed in a short dark skirt, and a silky, flowing blouse underneath a dark suitcoat. "Hey, Papi." She gives Armando a quick kiss on the cheek. Her shoes have high skinny heels that click on the wood floor as she crosses the room. "Sorry to be late. I've been trying to get ahead at work so I can take Friday off to get ready for the demonstration, and had to stay longer than planned."

She has a perfumed soapy scent, under laid with odors of coffee and bus exhaust.

Armando, his hand on Silvia's shoulder, says, "Molly, meet my daughter, Silvia Patricia. And this is María Molly, Corazón's daughter."

Molly nods and extends a hand, smiling broadly.

Silvia wears bright lipstick, has big dark eyes lined with eyeliner, and short dark hair that spikes out in spots. "It's so wonderful to finally meet you," she says as she releases Molly's hand. "Papi told us all about your adventures in the mountains. And it's so wonderful that you've reconnected—" she pauses a second, suddenly flushing "—well, anyway. Do you go by María or Molly?"

Somehow, the question makes Molly's breath catch. "Molly." Her voice sounds apologetic.

"Well, that's understandable, as you just barely reconnected with the Mexican side of your family, right?"

Now Molly's face flushes and I can smell her tension. "Yeah, um, right."

"But now that you and your mother are, uh, seeing each other again, have you thought about going back to María? Papi says that's what Cori called you when you were small. Embrace your Mexican roots?"

Benita leans forward, nodding. "That's how I know her—she'll always be María to me because that was her name as a baby."

Armando frowns. "Silvia," he warns in a low voice. "I don't think Molly needs your advice."

Silvia doesn't seem to have heard. Her eyes still on Molly, she says, "I think too many of us are ashamed, when we should be proud to be Latinas!"

Not sure what Silvia is talking about, but she's really upsetting Molly. I touch my nose to her hand and she grips my fur. Grips it a little hard, to be honest, so that it hurts, but I don't move away. Molly swallows. "My dad—" she begins, the color rushing to her face.

"Silvia," Armando says, his voice stern now. He gives his daughter a look much like the one my trainer Miguel would give us dogs when we were doing something he didn't want." He turns to Molly. "Silvia is an attorney who now works for the Department of Justice. She's one of the organizers of the demonstration this weekend."

"I only helped to organize it," Silvia says. "Didn't really do much. But I'll be giving a speech."

"And," Armando says, a little apologetically, "she's really into Latino rights."

Silvia bristles. "If every Latino and Latina would—"

"Silvia," Armando warns. "We're here to get to know Molly, not to talk politics."

Silvia glances at her father, an annoyed expression on her face. "It's not politics, it is our identity. Our life." But she falls silent.

For a moment, no one speaks. Then, Mariela says brightly, in that tone of false enthusiasm that the boss sometimes uses, "So, Molly, you go to a science immersion school? How you like it?"

Molly relaxes her grip on my fur, and I lie down at her feet. "It's a great school," she says. She talks about her classes, how she's also learning Spanish, which seems to make Silvia happy, but I've heard it all before, and I doze off.

I wake up to Cori's voice announcing dinner.

Chapter 18

Silvia

EVERYONE CROWDS AROUND CORI'S TABLE. ARMANDO holds Tony. Molly sits in between her mother and Benita.

Benita says a short prayer, just like the Franklins usually do before a meal, except here everyone but Cori, Molly, and Silvia move their hands across their chests at the end. I've seen people do that before, back when I attended some big churches as part of my service-dog training, but never at the Franklins, who just bow their heads.

And then everyone starts talking and eating and there's nothing for me to do but take a nap until they are finished. Since there's not much floor space with the extended table and the chairs, I sprawl in the doorway between the kitchen and living room.

I've barely settled, when I hear purring. Miga! She comes up to sniff noses with me. We exchange greetings, and then she curls up beside me. As I've said before, Miga is a very confident—one could even say uppity—cat, but we're friends now, so I don't mind.

Tony's voice awakens me. He's shouting something about cake. Miga has vanished. Armando, his voice raised to carry over his grandson's, says, "Two more bites and you can have cake." More wailing.

I sit up, my eyes on Armando. If he needs someone to dispose of a couple of bites of food, I'm ready and waiting.

After a good deal of protest, Tony finally manages to down the bites, although in the time he takes a dog could have cleaned up every plate on the table and polished off the contents of serving dishes as well. This kid needs eating lessons. Just sayin'.

I keep my eyes on the table, but unlike when I'm at Mrs. Franklin's, no one here puts food in a dish for me or gives me cake. And I don't think Molly remembered to bring kibble.

But trust Molly to come through. As she carries her dish to the sink, she asks her mother, "Can I give Doodle the scraps?"

Cori says yes, and gives her a paper plate to use, and soon I'm getting my own taste of Mariela's cooking. Beats kibble any day of the week.

Benita and Mariela go to the living room and Armando takes Tony outside. I follow him to the door, but he doesn't seem to see me. I don't really need to pee too badly, but a dog always likes to leave his mark, if you catch my drift.

"You're coming Saturday, right?" Silvia asks Molly as they start to load plates into the dishwasher. "To the Keep Our Children Home demonstration?"

"Maybe." Molly wipes her hand on a kitchen towel. "My dad might have plans, so we're not sure."

"But—" Silvia glances at Cori, who's drying a platter "—surely, if your father can't go, you could go with your mother?"

Both Molly and Cori freeze for a second, Molly holding a fork and Cori the platter.

Silvia turns to Cori. "You're planning to go, aren't you?"

Cori doesn't meet her gaze. "I'm not sure. I might have to work."

"But—" Silvia shakes her head in disbelief. "But—this demonstration is for *you*—for people like you. You've experienced how awful it is to have your parents get sent back to Mexico. And if you hadn't been old enough to stay, you, an *American* child, who lived here all your life, who knew nothing about Mexico— would have been forced to go live there. It could have happened to you. It's still happening to others, and unless we all stand up and fight for our rights, countless children will be deported."

Neither Molly nor Cori moves.

"I mean," Silvia says into the stony silence, "Molly, what would you feel if your father was told he had to leave the country and go to some strange place where you don't even speak the language and you had to go with him? That's what this is all about. We need to take a stand."

Whoa. Cori's lip tighten into an angry line. "Leave Molly alone," she says in a low voice. "Life isn't as simple as it might seem to you. Not for those of us who haven't had parents to hold our hand our whole life, to pay for college."

Silvia sucks in her breath, surprised. Her face flushes. "But this is your life," she says. "You lived it. That's what my speech is going to be about—how I and almost every Latina have personal experience with this terrible policy."

The platter makes a sharp sound as Cori sets it down forcefully. Fortunately, it doesn't break. She turns and glares at Silvia. "Don't you dare use my name or Molly's. Do you understand? It *is* my life. *My* life, not yours to parade in front of a bunch of demonstrators so you can feel good about your cause."

Silvia's mouth drops in surprise.

Cori, her black eyes furious, says, "You make it all sound so simple. Do this. Do that. And then it will all work out. Don't you understand it hardly ever works out no matter what you do? You dismiss my job like it's an inconvenience—something that gets in the way of being able to go to political rallies. You have no idea how hard I've worked to get where I am. No idea what I gave up—" she glances at Molly "—or how easy it could be to jeopardize it."

Silvia swallows, and moves a few steps back from Cori.

Uh-oh. Molly has tears in her eyes. I whine, and go over to touch her hand with my nose. All this tension makes me nervous, uncomfortable.

"It's okay, Doodle," she says under her breath.

"I'm not using names," Silvia says. "No one will know who I'm talking about."

"They *better* not," Cori says so severely that Silvia backs away even further.

And then, the back door flies open and Tony runs in sobbing, "Eeeva, Eeeva."

"He fell and scraped his knee," Armando says, "and thinks only Silvia can fix—" He stops, regarding Cori and Silvia who both stand stiffly, their faces flushed.

"Everything okay?" he asks, over the noise of Tony's cries.

Cori swallows, then says with another intense look at Silvia, "Yes. Everything is fine."

Tony twists his whole body towards Silvia, screaming, "Eeeva, Eeeva."

Silvia, with a final glance at Cori, turns her attention to the sobbing child. "Do you want your Eeeva?" she says in soothing tones. She holds out her arms, takes the child from a grateful

Armando, and walks toward the bathroom, saying, "Let's get this all better, okay?"

Molly, her hand trembling on my collar, says, "I'm going to take Doodle out."

We both hurry to the door, eager to escape the emotion in the room. Despite the tiny backyard, I find a good place to pee. By the time I'm finished and have sniffed around some, Molly seems less upset.

Cori is still in the kitchen, rinsing dishes, when we come back in. She gives Molly an apologetic smile and says, "I'm sorry about that. Families. Always a little drama, right?"

Molly smiles at this. "It's okay." She starts putting the dishes into the dishwasher.

I go into the living room where Benita is back in her chair, and Armando is taking a seat beside Mariela on the couch. No sign of Miga. Before long, Silvia returns, holding a now-quiet Tony. She walks over and sets him down by me.

Uh-oh. Should have stayed in the kitchen.

"Oggie," Tony says.

"*Perro*," she says, correcting him. "Say *perro*."

I might have mentioned before that I picked up a bit of Spanish with my second owner, the one I don't like to talk about. Mostly take-out food, but a few random words as well, *perro*, meaning dog, being one of them. Although, the way my second boss used it, usually when he was drunk and angry, the word always sounded like what the boss calls "language," and by that he doesn't mean Spanish.

Tony's face screws in concentration. "Eh-mo."

Silvia laughs. "No. *Perro. Peeeeh-rrrrrro.*"

"Eeeeeh-mmmo," Tony says again.

More laughter. Silvia tries several more times, with the same result.

The doorbell rings, the surprise once again making me bark. Usually I hear cars pulling into the driveway or footsteps coming up the porch long before anyone actually rings the bell. But it's hard to hear anything with Tony so close to my ears. Who now jumps away, pointing at me accusingly shouting, "Oggie loud! Oggie loud!"

Armando answers the door. Why, it's the boss! Now I feel a little embarrassed about barking. I rush over to greet him, as Armando says in a hearty voice, "Come in. Come in."

The boss looks a little flustered. "I don't need to. Just tell Molly that I'm here."

"She's helping with the dishes, which I think we should encourage." Armando gives the boss a big smile. "Come on in while she finishes and sit down. We don't see enough of you."

The boss, looking profoundly uncomfortable, takes a few steps inside, closing the door behind him.

Armando gestures towards the kitchen. "I'll tell Molly you're here."

"Thanks," the boss says. Silvia, her high heels clicking on the wood floor, approaches him. "You must be Molly's dad." She extends a hand. "I'm Silvia Vega. Armando's youngest daughter."

"Josh Hunter," the boss says, taking her hand briefly.

"I was just telling Molly how wonderful it is that you and Cori have, um, reconnected so Molly can know her mother's side of the family. It's just great." She beams at the boss, who stands stiff-shouldered looking as if he'd rather be somewhere—anywhere—else.

"Yeah," he says, without enthusiasm.

Silvia doesn't seem to have heard him. "And I was telling her about the demonstration this Saturday. At Lafayette Square. I'm going to be giving a speech—" another bright smile "—and I'm hoping it's going to be really good. But Molly said she might not be able to go?" She raises her eyebrows.

"We're not sure yet," the boss says. He rubs his beard.

"Because, with Molly's Latina heritage, plus everything you and Cori went through, I think she really deserves the chance to be there, you know? This is a part of her that it would be wrong to ignore."

Whoa. The boss's mouth tightens and he starts to flush, just like Cori earlier. Silvia seems to have that effect on people.

Armando, returning from the kitchen, says, "Molly says she's almost done. Won't you sit down?"

The boss rubs his beard. "I guess." He goes over to the couch and perches on the end closest to the door, looking ready to bolt. Tony toddles over and stares up at him.

Armando, still smiling, says, "This is my grandson, Tony. His parents, my oldest son Rodrigo and his wife Teresa, just moved here."

Tony pulls on the boss's knee. "Oggie loud." He points an accusing finger at me.

"Oh? Did he bark?" The boss looks amused, which is good because sometimes he gets annoyed when I bark.

"Oggie ark," Tony says. "Oggie loud."

"Doodle can be pretty loud," the boss agrees. Personally, I think he ought to reserve judgement as to just who is and who isn't "loud" until he's heard Tony scream.

Much to Armando's amusement, Tony seems to like the boss, and chatters at length at him, although I don't understand a word of what he's saying. From the look on the boss's face, neither does he.

Armando asks the boss about his business, and the boss in turns asks how Armando's restaurant is doing until Molly comes in from the kitchen, smelling of dish detergent. The boss jumps to his feet with relief, and after a round of hugs and goodbyes, we go out into the chilly night air and walk to the car.

When we're on the road, me in my crate and Molly in the front beside the boss, she asks, "What'd you think of Silvia?"

"Pretty intense."

"Yeah," Molly agrees. "But good with Tony. He loves her."

There is a long silence.

"She . . . she really wants me to go to the demonstration," Molly says at last.

The boss starts to tap on the steering wheel. "So she told me. Do you want to go?"

Molly says "Yeah, I think so. At least for Silvia's speech. She says it's going to be about . . ." she hesitates, "about, um, Mom's past. How her parents had to go back to Mexico."

Now the tapping on the wheel gets loud and the boss's neck stiffens. "She's going to talk about us?" he says sharply. "That's none of her business."

"Not by name. She promised Mom that she wouldn't give names. Just the situation. How it tore families apart."

"I definitely do not want to go and hear our past dredged up to make political points," the boss says. "What does your mother think of this?"

Molly sighs. "Same as you," she says in a small voice. "She was pretty angry. She told Silvia she'd better not use our names. But don't you think people should know that these things happen? Who wants to take kids away from the place they grew up in?"

"Now *you're* starting to sound like Silvia. God spare me idealists."

I'm not exactly following this conversation, except to feel the tension between them.

"But don't you think it's wrong? What happened to Mom?"

The boss shakes his head. "Of course I think it's wrong. Her family got a bad deal. But Molly, it's complicated. Remember that Cori's parents broke the law when they came here illegally. So, should people never have consequences for breaking the law? Some say yes, some say no. There are two sides to everything." Another shake of his head. "No, there are usually four or five sides to everything. People like Silvia make it sound so simple, like there's only one glorious, righteous way, which happens to be *their* way. But that's not life."

Molly doesn't answer and for a while we drive in silence. At last, she says in a thoughtful tone, "That's what Mom said, too. That Silvia makes everything sound simple when it isn't."

"There you go," the boss says.

Neither of them say anything for the rest of the way home, and when we get inside, the boss settles down at his computer. "Gonna get this homework done while it's still in my brain," he says.

Fortunately, Molly doesn't forget that I haven't really had dinner. She pours a can of kibble into my dish, and opens the fridge and takes a part of a slice of cheese and breaks it up over my food. This is why Molly is the greatest. The boss would never do that. Afterward, she takes me out to pee.

We come back in, and I settle down on my soft bed in the living room, ready at last to relax, when something truly awful happens.

Molly decides to practice her oboe. That oboe could give Tony a run for his money.

Chapter 19

Annie

WE GET HOME BEFORE IT'S TIME TO GO PICK UP Molly, because we only have two short jobs today, a motel we visit on a regular schedule, and a small rental home in south Arlington. The motel was bug free as usual, although two rooms had traces of pot and one reeked of cigarette smoke to the point that even the boss could smell it, which is saying something.

"Why do smokers feel they have the right to ignore no-smoking policies?" the boss asked, as we left, clearly irritated. Naturally, I didn't have an answer.

The south Arlington home, on the other hand, had such an infestation that I barely had my nose through the door when I smelled the bed bugs. The only question there was where to alert first. So many choices! Every room except the bathroom was teeming with the critters.

The boss doesn't like to do rentals when the tenants rather than the landlord schedule the visits, because often the landlord will refuse to pay, and the tenants can't afford us. But we do a fair number of them anyway. The boss calls it his charity work.

A report from us documenting that the place has bed bugs can give the renters, in the boss's words, "the legal ammunition they need to force their jerk of a landlord to clean up the place." He also likes to say that bed-bug bites "burn and itch as much for poor people as much as they do for the rich."

Today, however, we didn't, again in the words of the boss, "get stiffed." The owner turned out to be a woman who was appalled that the home was infested. "I just bought the place as an investment a month ago," she told the boss when he called her to report our findings. "I bet the former owners knew about the bed bugs. I'm going to call my lawyer to see if they violated disclosure laws."

"Those bugs have been there way longer than a month," the boss told her. "If they were termites, the walls would practically be falling down."

The landlady promised to send a check right away, which put the boss in such a good mood that he sang along with the radio all the way home.

So now the boss is doing paperwork and I'm napping on my bed in the living room. That is, until I hear the boss's keys jingle. I jump up, but the boss shakes his head and says, "You stay home and look after the place." Which means back to my nap, since there aren't any threats of intruders at the moment.

Both the boss and Molly are excited when they get home, and immediately start straightening up the house. No idea why, until, sometime later, the doorbell rings, and—whoa!—it's Annie, holding a large and extremely fragrant boxed pizza along with a six-pack of soda and two small bags.

Both Molly and the boss break out in goofy grins at the sight of her. I may have mentioned that Annie is one of our favorite people. She usually is wearing a baseball hat with her hair pulled back in a short ponytail, but today it's down, falling just past her shoulders.

"Thanks for calling and suggesting this," the boss says. "This will be a nice break in a hectic week."

Today wasn't anywhere near what I think of as "hectic," but I'm as happy to see Annie (and the pizza) as anyone.

Before long, Annie, Molly and the boss are all sitting at the kitchen table, paper plates in front of them, eating the pizza with gusto. I can't help but drool at the aroma. I know Molly's good to save me parts of her crust, and she usually throws in a bite or two that has cheese, so I sack out on the floor near the doorway to the living room while they all talk a mile a minute. Molly tells Annie all about the coming demonstration.

"It'll be my first time at Lafayette Square," she says, going on to spout all sorts of information about the park that she's learned from the computer.

After that, the boss and Annie talk about the workday they have planned for Saturday at Miguel's, helping to rebuild his barn. Then, Molly tells Annie about HEAR and how Dan went missing.

The boss wipes his mouth and puts the napkin on his empty plate and glances up at the clock above the stove. "Speaking of that, Madison's blog will be on in a few minutes. I think a certain budding photographer—" he tilts his head toward Molly "—might be featured."

Molly blushes and smiles shyly.

One good thing about pizza, besides the terrific flavor, is that the clean up afterward is easy. I get my kibble, and Molly comes through with some crust and a few cheesy bits, just as expected.

After she takes me for a quick trip outside, she settles on the couch while I stretch out on my bed by her feet. On the other side of her, the boss and Annie sit quite close together, looking up at Madison on the TV.

"Hi, y'all. Madison Greene here with the *Low Down News*, the blog that gives you the lowdown on the local news that matters to *you*.

"Last Sunday, we reported on the paint-bombing at the Arlington Dog Fest, noting that some unnamed sources suspected Humans for Enlightened Animal Relations, or HEAR might be responsible. Now, a source from the Arlington Police Department confirmed today that search warrants had been issued for several HEAR vehicles after photos from an unnamed source, taken in an Arlington neighborhood, showed possible evidence linking HEAR to the paint-bombs at the Arlington DogDays last week."

The screen changes from Madison's face to Molly's photo of the HEAR van.

"That's mine," Molly says.

"The *Low Down News* has acquired some disturbing images of the inside of a HEAR van, alleged to be implicated in the disappearance of a blind Jack Russell terrier from a west end Arlington neighborhood."

The screen changes to photos of Suzanne and the boy standing at the back of the van—just before they started chasing us. "Two suspects have been taken into custody."

Molly straightens up. "Those are all mine."

The photo changes to the inside of the van.

"—syringes and vials of phenobarbital, which are used to euthanize dogs and cats. This van was parked less than half a block away from where the Jack Russell, Dan, disappeared. The van also contained several paint grenades—" the screen changes again "—and a posted listing of dog events in the NoVa area including the Arlington DogDays."

"These were all mine," Molly says proudly.

Madison starts to talk about Mrs. Carter and suddenly the old woman's face fills the screen. "He never seemed to mind being blind," she says. "He was always a happy dog, ready for anything." She starts to sniff and the screen changes again to what looks like a giant office building.

"Madison must have interviewed her after all," Molly says.

The screen changes again, to a thin man with big-framed glasses, wearing a suit. "A spokesman for HEAR categorically denied any involvement in the disappearance of Mrs. Carter's dog, or in the paint-bombings at the Arlington DogDays."

The man leans into the camera, his face earnest. "There is no evidence connecting HEAR to any of this," he says. "Yes, we have euthanization equipment in our vans. If the public had to see some of the animals we see, animals in terrible pain, they would realize that sometimes giving an animal a peaceful, pain-less death is the most merciful thing we can do. We take on the difficult job of doing what is actually best for the animals that come under our care. Just as many citizens would prefer not to know what is sometimes required of our policemen or our military personnel in order to keep us safe, some naïve people would like to think that every pet born in America can live a happy, fulfilled life. Given our current pet populations, this is simply not feasible. And it cannot change as long as breeders continue to churn out more dogs than can be absorbed into homes, as long as people refuse to spay and neuter their pets."

Annie makes a clucking sound. "They hate breeders," she says.

His voice takes on an edge and he leans toward the camera. "And for those who think that no-kill shelters are the answer, I'd invite you to tour a few of them, to look at cage after cage of unadoptable pets who will spend their entire lives with the confines of a small pen and ask yourself if this is really the best solution."

Molly leans down and lays a hand on my head. "Is that true?" she asks, frowning in worry. "The dogs are stuck in cages forever?"

The boss seeing her face, turns down the sound.

Annie sighs. "I'm afraid so. As much as I don't like HEAR, I'm afraid I have to agree with him that no-kill shelters alone can't solve the problem. Too many dogs, not enough people, not to mention that many of the dogs are not adoptable, at least not by people who don't have considerable training skills."

She gives Molly a sad smile. "But the HEAR people are extremists. To say that sometimes euthanasia is the most merciful solution is one thing. To kill as many pets as HEAR does—they have over a 99 percent kill rate—is another. They don't try to find homes even for the adoptable ones. Not to mention they'd love to drum all breeders out of business if they could, and get rid of people owning pets."

Molly nods, solemnly. "Yeah, Suzanne said dog breeders were like Nazis."

The boss sighs, closing his eyes briefly. "Spare me idealists," he mutters.

"Exactly," Annie says, "I wouldn't have Chloe without her breeder. The good ones do a lot for dogs. So, HEAR is as extreme as the people who believe no one who loves dogs would ever euthanize one—just on the opposite end. Worse, I think."

The screen changes to a city street scene and Madison starts to talk about a proposed crosswalk. The boss taps the remote and the TV goes off.

"I bet they killed Dan," Molly says. "No matter what that man says. Like Mrs. Carter said, he didn't care that he was blind. He was happy. And now she's all alone."

Annie puts a hand on Molly's shoulder, and says with sympathy, "Poor woman. It's so hard to—" She stops abruptly, her eyes unfocused.

"What?" the boss asks.

"I just had a thought." Annie pushes her hair back from her forehead, still concentrating. "But I need to check it out before I say anything more."

Both the boss and Molly stare at her, puzzled. But Annie shakes her head, meeting the boss's eye. "I need some time. I wouldn't want to . . . promise anything I couldn't fulfill." She gives a glance so quick as to almost be imperceptible (at least to humans) at Molly, who looks thoroughly confused.

Annie stands and heads for the kitchen. "I'm going to make coffee," she announces in a suddenly cheerful voice. "I just happened to have brought dessert. Who wants brownies and—" she smiles down at me "—who wants a bone?"

I think we all know the answer to that! Soon, I'm gnawing on a very nice knuckle bone that still has bits of meat on it, while Annie and the boss are sipping coffee, and Molly is dipping her brownie in a glass of milk.

You can see why Annie is one of our favorite people!

Chapter 20

Demonstration

MOLLY PERCHES ON A CHAIR, WATCHING THE FRONT door like a border collie watches a ball. I'm on the floor next to her feet, wearing my no-pull harness because I get to go with her. She woke up earlier than usual, changed clothes several times, and gave me almost all of her cereal when the boss wasn't looking. Now we're waiting for Madison and Grady to pick us up.

"Did you know that Lafayette Park used to be called the President's Park, and it was part of the front lawn of the Whitehouse?" Molly has spent a lot of time on her computer reading about the park and, in her words, "catching up on history."

"I didn't," the boss says, slipping on one of his windbreakers.

"But then Jefferson thought the lawn was too big and while he was president, he had road builders cut Pennsylvania Avenue through it, so now it's a separate park."

I've never personally seen a lawn I thought was too big, but humans like tiny yards. Probably because they don't usually pee in them.

"And even though it's named after Lafayette, the statue in the center is of General Jackson. Lafayette's statue is on the southeast corner." Molly sighs happily. "I saw the Mall side of the White House on a class trip. Now, I'll see the other side."

"You and Grady will be sure to stay with Madison the whole time?" This isn't the first time the boss has asked this question, but, as I may have mentioned before, humans like to repeat themselves.

"Dad," she says. "I've already said I'll be careful and we'll stay with the adults."

The boss rubs his beard. "Just remember that in national parks like that, any kind of weirdo could be there."

He's already said this several times as well, during a long discussion over whether Molly should be allowed to go with Grady to the demonstration.

"Da-ad—"

"And keep a tight grip on Doodle's leash the whole time. I don't want my prime business asset lost on the streets of DC or getting hit by a car." The boss peers down at me. He's always worrying about how much I cost and whether or not I'll get lost. "I still wonder if it might be better to leave him here."

"He'd be in his crate too many hours," Molly says, reminding him of the point she's already made more than once. "And, if any weirdo comes around, Doodle can protect me."

Which I would. The boss thinks I would, as well, judging by the way his eyes soften when he glances down at me. "I can't say I wish I could go with you," he says after a bit. "The last thing I want is to hear a bunch of emotional speeches, everyone climbing onto their high horse."

There are going to be horses? First I heard about that. Molly calls herself horse crazy, but I'm not really fond of horses, myself. Too jumpy and unpredictable. Not to mention big.

"Besides," the boss adds, "Miguel is counting on me."

Normally, I'd go with the boss to Miguel's, but since the fire in his barn—that was an exciting night!—he doesn't want extra dogs at his place because, as he put it, "it's already a zoo here." That interested me, because zoos are a blast. I got to visit one in my service-dog-training days and loved seeing and, more importantly, smelling so many different animals. I've never known Miguel to have anything other than dogs at his place, but maybe that's changed.

At any rate, the boss had to decide whether to let me go with Molly or stay in my crate all day. No choice at all, as far as I'm concerned, but the boss can be a little dense about these things.

I hear Madison's van pull into the driveway before either the boss or Molly, my ears being far better. I give a little bark to alert them.

"She's here!" Molly jumps up and flings open the door.

The boss follows us outside, waving at Madison. "Be good," he says.

Molly opens the side door and the scent of Snippet, who's in her crate in the very back, mingling with a touch of perfume wafts out.

"We will!" Molly shouts, climbing into the van. She heaves the side door shut, buckles up, and we're off. I sit on the floor beside her because Madison's van doesn't have a crate for me like ours does.

"Did you bring your camera?" Madison asks Molly, without turning her head.

As one of my old bosses used to say, "Do birds fly?" Meaning, I think, that the answer is obvious, although I've seen a few birds that don't fly. One particularly huge and frankly scary bird comes to mind. I saw it the time we went to the zoo—that part, I remember now, was definitely not a blast. Birds should not be as tall as humans! And it had an evil eye, staring at me in a way that left no doubt it wanted to peck me with its enormous beak. If Miguel has a zoo, I hope it doesn't include birds like that.

"Yeah," Molly says. "And a spare battery and memory card."

"Wonderful," Madison says. "And if you'll let me look through them, I'll see if I want to buy any. Deal?"

"Deal." Molly's smile fills her whole face.

After a short drive, Madison says, "Well, here we are. Should we park on the Mall or Lafayette side? Either way, we'll have to walk some."

Walking sounds terrific to me, although Madison seems less enthused about the idea.

We drive some more, going very slowly, circling around the same area several times.

"I guess we'll park anywhere we can find a spot. We should have taken the metro," Madison mutters. "Or walked from Arlington. Or perhaps California. Probably would have been quicker."

"Dogs aren't allowed on the metro," Grady says.

"I know. That's why we're—there's one!" The van shoots forward and then veers sharply to the side. "Perfect," Madison says, pulling forward and then back, then forward again as she fits the van into the slot. "Well, closer would have been perfect, but at least it's a spot."

We walk down a long sidewalk near a busy road, with the fumes from the cars and buses pretty much drowning out other scents.

But then I catch a whiff of a sweet flowery scent, just as Molly says, "there's the park." As we get closer, she says, "Look at those trees! They're beautiful."

"Tulip magnolias," Madison says. "We had one in our yard when I was growing up. The smell of them always takes me back."

"The website called them saucer magnolias," Molly says authoritatively.

Madison gives her an amused look.

Molly, not appearing to notice, continues, "Lafayette's statue will be on our right, and the White House will be straight across the park." She points and there is indeed a big white house on the other side of the park, although a group of people, many of them holding large signs, partly block the view.

"I'd like to get a picture of Lafayette, if we could go there first." Molly pulls her camera from her windbreaker.

"Fine with me," Madison says. "I can always use a few shots of the park as setting."

We wait at a traffic light and cross a busy street, and then enter a park with wide brick walkways. Like most parks, this one has lots of trees, many not fully leafed out yet. Unlike most parks, this one has statues on every corner and a big one of a man on a horse in the center.

"Lafayette Square," Molly says, her voice filled with awe.

Snippet's excitedly alternating between sampling the air with her nose and lunging forward, nose to the ground.

"No pull," Grady says, giving a little jerk of the leash.

There's plenty to smell, that's for sure. So many different people, all kinds of exhaust fumes, grass, trees, and dogs. I don't see that many dogs here right now, but the shrubbery is well-marked with the scents of whole packs-worth of dogs. Is this a great place or what?

And then there are the squirrels. Tons of them. By the smell of it, maybe as many of them as people. And just as bold. Practically running underfoot. If I weren't on a leash . . .

"No pull," Molly says, jerking the leash a little. Oops.

A woman hurries towards us. Why, it's Silvia, waving and calling out, "Molly. Molly!" She's wearing dark tight pants under what looks like a bright belted shirt or maybe a short dress.

"You made it!" Silvia sounds a little breathless. Her face is flushed with excitement. She pulls Molly into a hug. "I'm *so* glad you're here! Look at the crowd!" She points to the group with signs clustered at the far end of the park. At least three hundred people, and more arriving all the time!"

Silvia bends down to pet me and Snippet. "Oh, Doodle, you have a friend." She glances at Grady and smiles and he nods back. "My parents are at Jackson's statue."

"The one on the horse in the center," Molly says, nodding, which gets another amused smile from Madison.

"Be warned. They have Tony." Silvia gives a mock grimace. "Oh, and my speech has been moved back to 11:30. Everyone thought we'd get better coverage then."

"You're giving a speech?" Madison asks, a friendly smile on her face.

"Yeah," Silvia says. "On how our current immigration policy hurts children."

Madison's eyes light up with interest. "And how do you know Molly?"

Molly gives a little jump. "Oh, I'm sorry." She waves an arm toward Silvia. "This is Silvia Vega. We're relatives . . ."

Silvia laughs. "Relatives is about as specific as we can get. I think of her as my niece but we're actually some kind of complicated once-removed or great-great cousins or something."

Molly gestures to Madison. "And this is Madison Greene and Grady. And Snippet. Grady and I go to the same school."

Madison holds out a hand as Silvia's eyes widen in surprise.

"Madison Greene? Not the blogger!"

"The one and only," Madison says, looking pleased.

"This—" Silvia shakes her head in wonder "—this is fantastic. Does this mean you're going to do a piece on Keep Children Home? That would be wonderful. We've been trying so hard to get the word out. It's such an important cause." She gushes on while Madison listens, looking mildly interested. "And if you include Molly's story, it'll be even better."

"Molly's story?" Madison snaps to attention like hound who's caught a scent.

Molly sucks in her breath and frowns at Silvia, who doesn't notice, her eyes on Madison.

"You know. How her mother's parents were deported. How her mother had to choose between staying here where she was a legal citizen, or going to Mexico, which was like a foreign country to her. Her mother's a living example of what we're demonstrating against here."

"No, I didn't know." Madison turns a calculating glance toward Molly.

"Mama," Grady says, in a low voice.

Molly, her face now flushed, says, "You're not going to use us in your speech are you? You promised you wouldn't. You promised." Her voice shakes on the word and she takes a big breath.

Silvia raises her hands as if fending off the barrage of words. "I didn't. Your mother's not in my speech. I just thought maybe Madison might be using it in *her* story." She gives Madison a hopeful look.

"First I've heard of it," Madison says. "Grady," she asks in a falsely cheerful voice, "did you know about Molly's, um, history?"

Grady, tight-lipped, shifts his weight from one foot to another. "Yeah, but I don't use my friends as news leads."

Molly turns to Madison. "My mom and my dad both would be *really* mad if you used them in your blog."

For a moment, the only sound is Snippet whining softly. I feel like whining myself, with all tension suddenly in the air. Madison stares at her son's face, set in a scowl, and then at Molly.

She puts a hand on Molly's arm. "Honey, I would *never* air anything your mama or daddy didn't want. Like Grady said, y'all are friends, not stories."

Molly and Grady both let out long breaths.

Madison turns to Silvia. "But I take it you would be willing to give an interview?" As Grady frowns, she hastily adds, "That doesn't include Miss Molly here?"

"Yes," Silvia says enthusiastically.

So, Molly takes Snippet's leash and leads us to a bench where we wait while Grady holds the camera on Silvia as she answers Madison's questions. Silvia's phone buzzes a couple of times while she's talking, but she ignores it. Behind us, where the demonstrators are, I hear excited voices. People start to move quickly away from the crowd by the fence. A short, paunchy man runs towards us. I jump up and watch, alert, since this isn't ordinary behavior. Silvia and Madison see him, too, and neither speaks as he approaches.

Grady pulls the camera away, but Madison motions for him to keep recording. He grimaces, but pulls the camera back to his face.

"Have you—" the man bends over and sucks in several quick breaths—"have you seen a kid, Latino, about two, dark hair? He's gone missing."

"Two?" Silvia asks. Her face pales. She whips out her phone and presses a key. "Mámi." She listens for a few seconds. "Okay. We'll cover this end. We'll search this area and work our way towards you. Molly's here and she can help. Don't worry. The park isn't that big. We'll find him." Her words sound confident, but her face looks stricken.

"Tony's missing," she tells us, her voice filled with alarm just as the out-of-breath man says, "Kid's name is Tony." She runs a hand through her hair. "He just disappeared. Mámi says one second he was standing by her, and then she turned and he was gone."

Molly jumps up, a leash in each hand. "Tony's her two-year-old nephew," she explains to Madison and Grady.

Madison says, "Have they contacted the park rangers? This place is crawling with federal agents. I can't imagine they won't be able to find him."

"I don't know." Silvia scans the park. "I saw one on the H Street entrance. I'll go ask him."

"And we'll cover the block between Pennsylvania Ave and H Street," Madison says. "I'll stay closest to the road, you two go further in—but stay close enough for me to see you. Ask everyone you see if they've seen him. Grady, keep filming. We might be able to use this!"

"I can't handle Snippet and the camera and search for the kid all at once," Grady complains.

Madison takes the camera from him. "Okay, you search." She pulls the camera up to her face, turning in a slow moving circle. Grady shakes his head, his lips tight.

"This is my *job*, Grady," Madison says, seeing his scowl. "It's how we got our new home."

Silvia angles off at a jog while the rest of us walk back toward the road we came in on. Molly shouts, "Tony. Toooo-ny," something lots of other people are doing as well.

"Can you find Tony, Doodle?" Molly asks in between calling out his name. "Can you smell him?"

I'm not exactly sure what she means, since she hasn't given me a scent to smell. When she says Tony, I remember the smell of urine and a small dark-haired kid shouting "Oggie." Is that who we're looking for? I work my nose as we trot along, but there are so many people running here and there, that there's little chance of catching a scent. Or even of hearing much, with all the shouts. We continue to walk back the way we came in, Molly and Grady calling out Tony's name. Madison walks along the street, alternately calling and stopping to shoot short videos.

Video cameras are every bit as mysterious as Molly's camera or her phone, in that I have no idea how holding a little gadget up to your face can end up being a movie on the computer, so that you can see something a second time exactly as it happened. Well, not exactly, because there's no scent on videos and there are certainly lots of scent here. And Molly often says she's shooting pictures or videos, but I've never seen a gun or heard any kind of bang. Puzzling, in the way many human things are.

And then, from the center of the park, comes a great cheers. Lots of people yelling and clapping. We all turn towards it. A muscular man with a shaved head runs over to us. "We found him!" he shouts, racing past us to shout the same thing at Madison, who once again has her camera up to her face.

Silva, her phone to her ear, catches up to us. "Thanks! That's wonderful!" She pockets her phone. "They found him," she says breathlessly. "He's fine. He had climbed into one of the fountains.

Good thing it doesn't have water yet this time of year! One of the demonstrators found him and took him over to my parents. They're all at Jackson's statue now." She hurries off and we follow after her.

It seems as if everyone we pass turns to us to say, "They found him! He's safe." There are a *lot* of people in the park right now, although, strangely, given all the dog scent, no dogs except a little terrier being held by an elderly man. Madison films many of the people making comments, which makes for slow progress as she keeps stopping to hold out the camera. "This will be the feel-good story of the week," she proclaims happily.

And then, Molly raises her head and waves. "There they are!" She breaks into a jog and soon we come up to Armando and Mariela standing in front of a fence that circles a statue of a man on a horse. Mariela holds Tony, as he sobs into her shoulder. Silvia pats him on the back, talking to him in soothing tones.

"Lost," Tony sobs, burying his head into Mariela's shoulder. "Ony lost."

Mariela, looking near tears herself, shakes her head. "One second he had my hand and the next he was gone. My daughter may never let us take him anywhere again."

Armando raises an eyebrow. "And that would be so terrible?" But he smiles as he says it.

Molly, grinning as well, waves at Grady and Madison, and when they catch up to us, introduces them to Armando and Mariela. "Silvia's parents," she tells Madison, who immediately asks them if she can do a short interview. When Mariela frowns, Madison quickly adds, "Just a few shots of your grandson—is it Tony?—safe in your arms. I'm doing a piece about how great everyone here was in helping to search for him."

She hesitates. Armando asks, "Nothing political?"

"Nothing political. All feel-good stuff," Madison assures him.

Mariela's shoulders relax, and she gives Madison a tired smile. "I guess that'll be okay. People have been wonderful. I can't believe how quickly everyone acted to search for him."

Silvia gives Tony a kiss on the head, and then smiles at the group. "Gotta go. My speech is in fifteen minutes. Don't miss it!" She strides off toward the group of people holding signs.

"Grady, will you do the honors?" Madison asks, holding the camera towards him.

"Sure." He doesn't look particularly enthusiastic.

Madison smiles at Mariela. "I'm between cameramen right now, and Grady's filling in." She beams at him, proudly. "He's really quite good."

"Maybe he will become a journalist like you," Armando says.

Grady looks alarmed at the suggestion, but takes the camera.

Armando pulls out his phone and starts to walk away. "I'd better call his parents so they don't find out about this on the evening news."

Molly takes Snippet's leash and points. "We'll be over there, where we can sit down." She leads us along the fence circling partway around the statue to a bench. She sinks down on the seat. Snippet and I stretch out at her feet.

I lay my head down, my nose assaulted with squirrel scents. I don't think there's a single blade of grass in this park that doesn't smell like the creatures. Can't say that's a good thing.

Molly checks her phone. "Thirteen minutes till—"

A voice interrupts her. "Molly! Moooollly."

Why it's Hailey, half running towards us from the group of demonstrators at the fence facing the big white house.

She comes up to us, her eyes red and swollen, smudged with streaks of black makeup. Her hair sticks our wildly around her face. Her cheeks are tear-stained, her expression frantic. "I'm so glad to see you!" She plops down on the corner of the bench, and turns toward Molly. "Maybe you can help."

Chapter 21

Drop Off

I'M REALLY SCARED," HAILEY SAYS, BITING HER LOWER lip.

"What's wrong?" Molly leans forward, her eyes dark with concern. "Are you alone?"

"You know how Hershey disappeared from the dog fair?"

Molly nods.

"Well, I was right. He was stolen. I got a call. A man's voice. He said if I wanted Hershey back I had to come to the demonstration today and bring $300."

"Ransom!" Molly breathes in amazement.

Hailey nods vigorously. "I told you he was stolen. This man said at 11:30 exactly—" she glances at her phone "—I'm supposed to put the money in a Wendy's paper bag that will be on the park bench to the right of the fence in front of the White House."

She points at the crowd of demonstrators clustered between us and the long white house on the other side of the street. "Then I'm supposed to go straight through the park and cross H Street without looking back, and wait on the H Street side of

St. John's church. He said if I looked back and tried to see who picked up the bag, I'd never see Hershey again."

"Wow." Molly shakes her head. "When did he call?"

"About a week ago, which was good, 'cause it took me some time to get the money."

Molly tilts her head in surprise. "Get the money? Didn't you just ask your parents?"

"No!" Hailey sounds alarmed at the idea. She pushes her hair back from her face. "They don't know I'm here. They wouldn't let me come here alone. I'm supposed to be at Alisha's. She's a good friend. We cover for each other. My parents wouldn't pay ransom and anyway, I can't tell them." She starts to cry again.

"What?" Molly asks. "Why can't you?"

"Because they think Dominga did it. You heard my mom at the park, saying how suspicious it all was. She thinks Dominga arranged it because my mom—" her lip trembles and Hailey shudders in silent sobs, then sucks in a shaky breath "—because my mom told her a few weeks ago she was letting her go." Hailey's eyes are full of accusation. "She *fired* Dominga and never told me. She was just going to have her disappear like every nanny I've ever cared about has done my whole life." She swallows and says, tears streaming down her face, "I *hate* her."

"I'm sorry," Molly says softly. She puts a hand on Hailey's arm. "I'm so sorry."

"So I can't ask my mom for the ransom." Hailey's face contorts in anguish. She whispers, "What if my mom's right? I don't think Dominga would do it—she knows how I love Hershey— but what if she was mad and . . ."

"She wouldn't do it," Molly says firmly. "She wouldn't do that to you."

Hailey shakes her head. "That's what I thought. But . . . but . . ." She swallows hard. "The guy who called about the ransom? He had an accent. Spanish." She swipes a hand across her face and says dejectedly, "If it was Dominga, I don't want my mom to find out. You know? Because Mom would just say that's the kind of people immigrants are—she's always going on about that kind of stuff—and she would have Dominga arrested in a heartbeat." Her eyes well with tears again.

"I don't think your mom—"

"You don't know her," Hailey insists. "First, she says Dominga needs to be fired because she had to have been in on it. Because she . . . she's the one who suggested we tie up Hershey. But that was because she didn't want me in the restroom alone." Hailey reaches into a pocket, pulls out a tissue, and blows her nose.

"When I asked my mom why on earth Dominga would do that, would jeopardize her job, which she *loves*—" she bends closer to Molly, as if trying to prove a point "—Dominga's said lots of times she loves the job. That she loves *me*." She gives Molly a fierce look as if daring her to disagree. "Then my mom tells me she'd already told Dominga they were going to let her go at the end of the month. She believes Dominga arranged to steal Hershey as revenge. Which means the whole 'we're firing her because she stole Hershey' is a joke. No. A lie."

Hailey draws in a shaky breath and says, her voice hard with accusation, "She was going to get rid of her anyway. Without telling me. Like she always does whenever I start to really like my nannies. She's a witch and I *hate* her."

Snippet whines. I have to admit I feel like doing so myself. Too much emotion.

"It'll be okay," Molly says softly.

"But it won't." Hailey swipes a new tissue across her eyes. "Mom fired her and now I won't ever see her again. That's how it works, you know? When nannies get fired, they can't stay in contact with their kids, even when they still love the kids. What if she has to go back to El Salvador? It's like a death trap over there. She could get killed." Her face contorts as she starts to cry, her body heaving with each sob.

For a moment, Molly shakes her head slowly. Then she ties my leash to one of the bench slats, does the same with Snippet's, and slides over to put an arm around her, as Hailey continues to cry. "It's like losing your mother, you know?" Hailey says in a thick voice. "She was more a mother to me than my own stupid mom. She loved me. Who'd take a mother away from her child? I'll never have a real mom to be with me, you know?"

Molly goes rigid for a second and swallows. "I know," she whispers in a voice so soft that I'm not sure if Hailey can hear it. But the sadness in Molly's voice makes me stretch out my neck to lick her hand.

When Hailey stops crying and pulls away, Molly scans the park anxiously. "So what are you going to do? Give the ransom yourself? It could be dangerous."

Hailey nods. "I know. I'm scared. But what can I do?"

Molly straightens up. "My mom's a cop. She could come do it for you. She lives in Alexandria and—"

"No!" Hailey gives her a panicked look. "She'd have to tell my parents. Cops always have to tell the parents."

Just then Snippet jumps up, startling me. She pulls at the end of the leash, tail wagging because, hey, here comes Grady, hurrying towards us.

"Mama says it's almost time for Silvia's—" he stops, his eyes on Hailey. "What's going on?"

"*Grady's* here?" Hailey looks like a shelter dog who gets her cage door opened. "He could do it."

"Do what?" Grady asks, suddenly cautious.

Molly, her voice low, tells him about Dominga's being fired and the ransom request from a man with a Spanish accent.

"Could you do it? Put the money in the bag? And maybe Molly and I could go to the church and wait, and you could see who picks up the money."

Grady considers it. "Yeah, I guess." He thinks some more. "Three hundred dollars?" he asks. "Doesn't seem like much."

"It's enough. I had to use my card to get some of it, and borrow the rest from a friend. My parents will have a fit when they get the statement." She bites her lower lip. "But, yeah, I see what you mean. Hershey cost over a thousand. Good thing he didn't ask for that."

Snippet has been tugging at the leash, impatient to get to Grady, and now she starts to bark. "Hey, girl," Grady says, smiling. He unties her and Snippet waggles her butt in happy greeting. "No jump." He bends down to pet her.

Molly frowns. "It doesn't make sense to have Grady put it on the bench. You need to do it, in case the guy is watching, so he can see that you're going straight to the church without looking behind you. And Grady and I can just kind of lurk around and see who shows up for the money."

Hailey thinks about it for a second. "Grady could wait for them and you could come with me." She gives Molly a pleading look. "I don't want to be alone."

"They might not like seeing two people at the drop," Grady says.

Molly squints in concentration. "I suppose I could go wait back here a bit, and then join you on the walk to the church."

Hailey grabs one of Molly's arms. "Would you? That's be great. I . . . I don't want to be alone," she repeats.

At that moment, Madison comes walking briskly towards us, waving and shouting. "Come on, y'all. Can't miss Silvia's big moment."

Grady, Molly, and Hailey all freeze for a second.

Then, Grady says, "Coming!"

"Silvia?" Hailey asks blankly, while Molly's untying my leash.

"My, um, cousin," Molly says. "She's giving a speech."

We all troop behind Madison who walks briskly to the edge of the crowd, which has grown considerably. Lots of people jostling about, and, despite the cool weather, a fair assortment of interesting body odors, not to mention feet of all sizes to sniff.

"There it is," Hailey whispers, darting a glance at a bench that has two people on each end and a fast-food bag in the middle.

A small platform has been set up next to the fence separating the park from the road and the big white house beyond it. There are a couple of big signs on the platform and several mike stands.

Hailey checks her phone. "Eleven-twenty-five," she says in a low voice.

Molly, her face skewed in concentration, glances at Madison, who has her camera out and is already busy scanning the crowd. Grady shifts his weight from one foot to another.

Molly asks Madison in a strained, fake-cheerful voice, "Is it okay if we go over to those park benches? We could stand on them and see better. All I can see from here are heads." She stands on tiptoe, stretching out her neck to demonstrate, but Madison doesn't look her way.

"That'll be fine," Madison say, camera still to her face. "Y'all just don't go anywhere, okay? I'm going to see if my press card can get me in a little closer, then I'll meet you after the speech." She lowers the camera and threads her way in between a bulky man holding a big sign and two gray-haired women wearing shawls around their shoulders.

There's a grating squeak—that awful sound that mikes often make—and then Silvia's voice booms, "Hola, amigos! I'm gratified and overwhelmed to see such a crowd here. I want to thank each one of you for showing up today to protest the U.S. government's inhumane deportation policy . . ."

Molly says to Hailey, "You put the money in the bag, and then head straight toward General Jackson's statue. I'll wait, and catch up to you on the other side of the statue."

"And I'll just kind of mingle with crowd here, and keep an eye on the money," Grady says. "And whoever takes it."

"Eleven-thirty," Hailey says, her voice tight with tension. She pushes her hair back from her face, swallows, straightens her shoulders, and then walks head high over to a bench behind and to the side of us. At one end, a tired looking woman in jeans and a sweater, both tight, wrestles with a toddler on her lap. At the other, what looks like a homeless person, wearing mud-stained work boots and bundled up in a long old over-coats, sits, head down. A visor cap pulled down low under a dark hoodie and large sunglasses hide the person's face.

"Is that our man?" Grady whispers.

"Can't tell," Molly says.

In fact, without any scent, it's impossible to know whether the sleeper is a man or a woman.

After a brief look around, Hailey walks over to the bench, picks up the sack and quickly drops a small package wrapped in plastic inside it. Then she casually places the bag back on the bench. She glances at the woman and the sleeping man, sighs, then resolutely turns and hurries away.

"She's got guts," Grady says, "even if she is always an emotional wreck."

"Yeah," Molly agrees. "Gotta go. You want me to take Snippet?"

Grady shakes his head. "No. I'll look more like one of the crowd if I have her."

Molly and I take off after Hailey, heading toward the statue of the man on a horse. She walks right past the figure on the bench, close enough that I turn my head to sniff at the hooded figure. Ah. Definitely male. A teenaged boy. Not that anyone could tell from looking, the way he sits with his face to his chest. Which is why the nose is always better. The nose never lies!

"Doodle!" Molly whispers, giving the leash a little jerk. I straighten and keep my head near her side in a proper heel. Molly walks quickly, not turning her head at all. I smell at least three different squirrels, but she never slows down, jerking the leash again the few times I try to investigate the scents.

The park is more crowded than earlier, and in addition to squirrels, offers up scents of all people we pass. Most are going the opposite direction, toward the demonstration. We pass several families carrying signs, parents holding the hands of small children, an old woman under a thick pile of blankets in a wheel chair being pushed by a skinny man in shorts. I stay by Molly's side but work my nose to take it all in.

Hailey is waiting for us on the back side of the statue. An Asian man stands with one arm around a woman, the other holding out a long stick that has his phone attached to it. Very odd, the way he's grinning at it.

"You go ahead and cross at the light and I'll catch up. Just in case anyone's watching you leave the park," Molly says. "Although there are enough people here, I'm not sure I'll be noticed."

Hailey nods, white-faced and takes off, almost at a run. We follow more slowly, down the broad brick walkway until we pass between some iron posts a little taller than I am and come to a busy intersection. All the cars are coming from the same direction. Molly presses a button on a street light pole. A bus rumbles by, spewing out its distinctive sharp odor, whining to a stop a little beyond us to let several people on. I know about buses and bus stops from my service dog training, of course, and they can be rich areas to find bits of food. Although with all these squirrels, I doubt there's a morsel of food in the whole park.

Between us and the bus stop, on our side of the road, is a squat white building that, after only a few whiffs, I realize must be a restroom. On the other side of the street is a church, looking kind of small in the midst of so many other big buildings.

Molly's phone buzzes, and she pulls it out of her pocket, studying the screen. The pole starts to beep with the signal to go—another thing I learned about in service-dog school. People are always talking about red and green lights, but to be honest, I often find it hard to tell the difference, so I wait for the sound.

With a little start, Molly shoves her phone in her pocket and we cross the road. We don't go to the front of the church, which faces a cross road and has pillars and a big porch, but turn and walk a little ways down the busy sidewalk. We find Hailey sitting on some steps leading up to a small door on the side of the church.

"Any news?" Hailey asks, as Molly sits down beside her. I sit, too, in my usual way with stairs, with my butt on one level and front paws on the next step below.

"Grady just texted. He said the guy—he's pretty sure it was a guy—in the big coat and hoodie got up and took the sack, looked all around, and then disappeared into the crowd. He couldn't follow with Snippet. So he's waiting, watching to see if the guy comes out again. He didn't see anyone with a dog like Hershey."

"What if they don't keep their promise?" Hailey's voice holds the threat of more tears.

"We have to give them time," Molly says.

Neither of them talk after that, but both keep checking their phones and watching the street.

Finally, Molly's phone buzzes again. She stares at the screen. "The guy came out of the crowd—he ditched the coat and hat, but Grady recognized the hoodie and sunglasses and the boots—and he's heading for the church!" she says in an excited voice. "Grady's going to follow at a distance."

"Did the guy have Hershey?" Hailey asks.

"I don't think so or he would have said."

Hailey bites her lip, then studies Molly, her eyes wide with worry. "Maybe he's coming to check if I'm alone before he gets Hershey. What if he sees you and doesn't bring Hershey because I'm not alone?"

Molly sighs. "I could go back across the street and wait."

Hailey gives a quick nod. "Then he could see I'm alone."

"Okay," Molly says, standing up. "Maybe I can get a good look at him. Or a photo." She leads me back to the corner, running a little as the light has just changed and the beeping has started.

We catch up to an older man with a sunken face, who smells like cigarettes and whiskey. As we cross, a frizzy-haired woman in sparkly sandals, barges past us, head bent to her phone and talking loudly.

Molly stops when we get to the curb and checks her phone. "Nothing," she mutters. Then, looking straight ahead, toward the statue, she stiffens and sucks in her breath. The loud woman is still walking and talking, but Molly's staring at a thin figure in dark hooded sweatshirt jogging towards us. He looks like the guy on the bench—same sweatshirt and big sunglasses—but he's too far away for me to catch his scent. And just as he's finally getting closer, he veers off the main path toward the restrooms, running around them at the far side, and then slowing and walking to the bus stop.

Molly lets out her breath and quickly types into her phone. Across the street, Hailey pulls out her phone, and glances up at us, before quickly looking away.

Hey! Here come Grady and Snippet towards us. I'm not sure if Molly sees them, because she turns toward the bus stop and starts to walk, without a glance in their direction.

And then, everything seems to happen at once.

A dog, held on a leash by a kid—also wearing sunglasses and a hooded sweatshirt, but this one light colored—barrels around the corner at the far end of the church.

"*Hershey!*" breathes Molly, rigid with attention. She fishes her camera out of her pocket.

"Hershey!" Hailey calls out.

I can't tell whether it's Hershey or not with all the car fumes between us and the dog, not to mention the air is made worse by a bus that suddenly passes, momentarily blocking my view.

Across the street, the boy comes up to Hailey, who leaps to her feet. He tosses the leash at her, and then bolts across the road. He waves at the bus, just as the guy in the dark sweatshirt hops on.

"Hershey!" Hailey lunges at Hershey, trying to grab his leash, but—maybe because she sounds so upset—he shrinks out of reach. He hesitates for a second, looking from Hailey to the kid.

Then, just as the light changes, Hershey bounds into the street.

Chapter 22

Explanations

"Hershey!" Hailey screams. She runs into the road, then backs to the curb as a car passes. "Hershey, *come*!"

"He's going to get hit!" Molly starts toward the dog, then stops with a little moan, looking down at me. She waves the hand holding the camera at the cars moving through the intersection, crying, "Stop! Stop!"

The kid, almost to the bus, turns and stares at Hershey loping towards him. "Go back!" he yells.

"Hershey, *come*!" Hailey shouts.

But Hershey, now closer to our side than Hailey's, shows no sign of hearing. A car brakes hard when Hershey runs in front of it, the driver honking the horn.

Hershey jumps at the sound, his tail sinking between his legs. He slows, eyeing cars nervously as if seeing them for the first time.

"Stupid *dog*!" The kid runs back into the street, gesturing to the oncoming cars, weaving through them. He grabs Hershey's leash and leads him back to our side of the road, waving at the driver as he passes in front of the bus.

"Wait!" he cries.

He runs straight to us. "Take him!" He thrusts the leash at Molly. She misses it, but quickly bends down and grabs it, sucking in her breath in surprise as she straightens up. I sniff, and catch a bit of scent, but it's overwhelmed by bus fumes. The boy races back toward the bus, but it is already pulling away.

"No!" he cries, sounding near tears. He turns and darts past us, chasing after the bus.

"No!" Molly says to Hershey, who tugs on the leash trying to follow. "Hold still," she mutters, as she aims her camera at the fleeing boy and clicks it a bunch of times.

At the corner, the bus makes it through the next intersection before the light changes, but the boy, farther behind, doesn't. Instead of following the bus, he turns and crosses the street.

Hershey barks, still straining against the leash. Molly gives it several hard yanks, her gaze on the boy. When he disappears down the next street, she straightens up and calls out to Hailey. "Hershey's fine! I got him."

Hailey points to the intersection where we crossed earlier, already hurrying toward it. "I'm coming."

Molly and I and Hershey make our way toward the crosswalk. It's slow going because Hershey, recovered from his earlier panic, tries to greet every person we pass.

"No *pull!*" Molly says through gritted teeth, giving the leash a few more pops. She looks up with relief when Grady and Snippet come up to us. "How she ever thought Hershey could pass the good citizen test—"

"Let me help. I'll take him and you take Snippet," Grady says.

Molly trades leashes. "Thanks!" she says, her voice grateful.

"Snippet is a thousand times better. Did you see what happened? With that kid? I think I know who did—"

Grady's phone beeps. "Hey," he says, checking it. "Mama," he mouths to Molly as he lifts the phone to his ear. "Yeah, I found them and we're on our way back." I can hear fragments of Madison's voice, but then Hershey drags Grady toward a woman with glistening skin who smells like sunscreen. "Gotta go," he puffs. "We'll be there soon."

He reels in Hershey. "Stupid dog," he says, shaking his head, but his voice not angry. "You could have been smashed on the pavement." He turns to Molly. "What were you saying?"

Molly looks back down the street where the boy disappeared. "I . . . I'm not sure."

When we get to the corner, Hailey waves to us from the other side of the crosswalk.

Grady leans towards Molly and says in a low voice, "We've got to get back. Mama was about to call the cops to search for you. I told her you and Hailey went to take photos of the other monuments, and you were okay because you were together, and she said, 'With Hailey? I don't think how you could imagine a gnat could be safer with that girl than by itself.'"

Molly smiles briefly at this, and then the traffic signal beeps, and soon Hailey is rushing up to us. "Hershey!" she cries, bending to throw her arms around him. "Oh, Hershey! I was so scared." She carries on, petting and kissing and hugging him, until finally Grady says, "We really need to get back."

"Okay." Hailey straightens up. "Thank you both *so* much. I don't know what I would have done without you."

We all take off at a brisk pace—well, brisk for humans—back

toward the podium and the demonstrators. Hershey, for once, trots beside Hailey without pulling.

For a moment, no one speaks. Then, Hailey suddenly turns to Grady. "You can't tell your mom what happened. You know she'll put it on the web and then I'll be in *so* much trouble. You *can't* tell her. *Please?*"

Grady frowns, his eyes on the brick path, but finally says, "Okay. So what *are* we going to tell her?"

"The photo story?" Molly says. "She knows I always want to take more."

"Photo story?" Hailey asks.

Molly explains, stopping for a second to pull her camera out and click a few shots of the man-on-horse statue as we come up to it. "So I actually have some," she explains.

"But what are we going to say about how I got Hershey?" Hailey asks, as we round the statue.

Before anyone can answer, Madison comes bustling up to us, her mouth set in a hard line and her eyes angry. She glares at Molly. "Where in God's creation have you been?"

"Mama, I told you—" Grady begins, but his mother interrupts him.

"And *I* told you *both* not to go anywhere but the park bench. Is that not correct?"

Molly nods mutely while Grady says, "Yes, ma'am."

Still glaring at Molly, Madison continues, "Your daddy will never let me take you so far as the end of the block if he hears about this. If I tell you to be one place—" she moves her gaze to include Grady "—you both need to be at that *exact* spot and not one *inch* further away. Is that understood?"

Another nod and "Yes, ma'am."

"And if—" Madison is interrupted by Hershey, who lunges forward, half-dragging Hailey, and jumps up on her.

"Off!" Madison and Hailey shout simultaneously.

Hailey drags Hershey back. "Down," she commands in a severe tone. Hershey sits, panting.

Madison looks at the dog as if seeing him for the first time. "You got him back?" she asks, clearly surprised.

"Yeah, isn't it great?" Hailey suddenly sounds more nervous than happy.

"How'd that happen?" Madison peers down at her with sudden interest.

Molly stiffens and I feel her tension through the leash.

"Um, it just kind of . . ." Hailey casts a desperate glance at Grady.

Molly swallows. "She got a phone call from the thieves saying they were sorry they took him, and if she came to the park here, they'd return him."

"They?" Madison asks. "There was more than one?"

"Oh." Molly's face flushes and she stammers, "He. I just said 'they' but it was just some guy, right?" Now she's the one looking desperate.

"Just one guy," Hailey says firmly. "So I took the metro here, and I asked Molly to be with me because—" she gives Madison a knowing glance "—I know better than to be by myself with strangers, and we met on the corner. She points to where we just were. "And this guy just came and gave me Hershey."

"Just gave him to you?" Madison asks dryly.

Hailey beams up at Madison, looking pleased with herself. "I think he was worried with all my dad's connections—you know he's *really* high up in the State Department?—that he'd get caught and be in big trouble. The guy told me if I promised there'd be no *publicity,* he return Hershey, no harm no foul."

Madison raises an eyebrow, looking completely unconvinced. "Really? He steals the dog and then just decides to return him out of the goodness of his heart? Or—" she fixes Molly with a stare "—*their* hearts?"

"His," Hailey says hurriedly.

Madison shakes her head in disbelief. "It's a freakin' Christmas miracle."

Christmas? I thought that was still far away. Confusing. Maybe to Grady as well, because he Molly exchange an alarmed look.

"And what did this goodhearted guy look like?" Madison asks.

Hailey shakes her head. "I don't know. He was wearing some sort of hoodie and I couldn't really see him. Bulky man. Tall."

This surprises me because I only saw a skinny teenager and a skinnier kid.

Hailey says, "But I *promised* him there'd be no publicity. So you can't use this on your blog."

Madison raises both eyebrows at this, and her lips press together. Then she sighs. "Well, then." Another pause. "Let's get home."

"Home?" Molly looks towards the podium and demonstrators. "Can we go back just for a minute? So I can say goodbye to Armando and Mariela?"

Madison shakes her head. "Honey, that ship is way *way* out on the deep blue sea. They wanted to tell you goodbye, but their grandbaby was fussy, and when Grady told us you were on the other side of the park, they decided to leave."

Molly's face sags and I feel her disappointment through the leash.

Hailey also seems distressed by this news. "You're leaving?" She glances around a little wildly. "I'll be alone." When Madison says nothing, Hailey, a pleading tone coming into her voice, asks, "Is there any chance you could give Hershey and me a ride home? My mom's at a meeting and my dad's out of town until late tonight. I . . . I didn't think about how we'd get home when I took the metro here. Dogs aren't allowed." She pushes back her hair and flashes Madison an apologetic smile. "So, I'm kind of stranded."

Madison frowns. "Three dogs in the car . . ."

"I'd be here all alone," Hailey says, her voice much like a dog whining for a treat.

With another sigh, Madison resumes walking. "I guess. Come on, then."

"Great!" Hailey says. "I live in the Executive Court Apartments, over on 26th. You can drop us off in front. That'll be perfect. And remember, you can't use this on your blog."

"Yes, ma—am." Madison adds enough edge to that drawn out word that all of us dogs as well as Grady and Molly glance up at her.

Hailey doesn't seem to notice. As we walk, she happily rambles on about all the things she's going to do with Hershey now that she has him back again.

When we get to Madison's van, it takes a moment to figure out who goes where. Hailey announces that she gets car sick if she sits in the back, so she takes the front seat. Molly and Grady share the back seat, Snippet and me at their feet, which is pretty crowded, especially for Grady as he's tall. Hershey ends up in Snippet's crate, in the very back.

Even Hailey seems to have run out of things to say, so, other than her directions to Madison as to where she lives, we all ride in silence.

Finally, she points to a high-rise building that seems all glass and steel. "Those are ours on the right, over there. There's an unloading place by the office." Madison turns into a short road that takes us under an awning in front of large glass double doors. "Thanks again," Hailey says, as she lifts the back door to let Hershey out. Grady gets out so he can put Snippet in Hershey's place, and then goes to sit up front.

As we watch Hershey tug Hailey toward the big sliding doors, Madison says, "I'll confess that I'm a mite tired of our Miss Hailey."

"Total high maintenance," Grady agrees, as the car merges back on to the street.

Without turning her head, Madison says in a steely tone, "Now, will you two tell me what *really* happened today? Because if I believe that sweet fairy tale Miss Hailey told me, then I'll have to quit journalism and, oh, I dunno, maybe go into astrology or something. Or sell aluminum siding."

A baffling statement, to be sure, but Molly and Grady seem to understand it.

Grady says, "She made us promise not to tell."

"Because it could get her in trouble," Molly adds. "With her parents."

"I'm not her parents," Madison says firmly. "And *you*, Grady Jefferson Greene will be in big trouble with *your* parent if you don't tell me."

"Are you asking me to go back on my word?" Grady asks. "Because you always say—"

"I know, I know." Now, Madison sounds angry. "A Greene never goes back on his—or her—word." She drives for a while in silence. Finally, she says, "If y'all can assure me that nothing went on that was illegal or immoral . . ."

"Nothing immoral," Grady says quickly.

"And *we* didn't do anything illegal," adds Molly, earnestly. "I don't think Hailey did either. It's just that Hailey's parents will be angry. And she made us promise . . ."

"No one *makes* you promise anything," Madison snaps. She slows the car and then pulls into a gas station parking lot, parking off to the side. She takes her hands from the wheel and turns to look first Grady and then Molly in the eye.

"Did you do *anything* that will put *any* of you—including that high-strung prima donna—in danger? Because danger *must* trump promises made just to keep her out of trouble. Understood?"

They both nod. "Nothing," Grady says fervently, echoed by Molly.

"All right, then." Madison eases the car to the driveway and back onto the street. "Every dog has his secrets."

Really? I'm not totally clear on the concept of secrets, but I'm pretty sure it's not a dog thing.

No one speaks a word until Madison pulls into her driveway. Her garage door goes up all by itself, which is a little unnerving.

Molly and Grady take us dogs straight to the backyard, where we get long drinks before sniffing along the perimeter of the yard. No intruders other than birds, which, sad to say, we can't do anything about. So we stretch out on the grass to let the sun's warmth soak through our fur deep into our bones. I have a wonderful nap and don't wake up until I hear the boss's van pull into the driveway.

Chapter 23

An Unhappy Discovery

MOLLY LOADS ME INTO MY CRATE, EVERYONE SAYS goodbye, and then we're backing out of the driveway.

"How'd it go?" the boss asks Molly as we ease out onto the street. "Was Silvia's speech a success?"

"Yeah, great," Molly says with such false enthusiasm that I'm surprised the boss doesn't notice, except he doesn't seem to be paying much attention.

"Good," he says, sounding distracted. After a few minutes, he says, "Thought we could pick up some burgers for dinner."

"Zeke's?" Molly asks, suddenly excited. For good reason, too. Zeke's Burgers is Molly's and my favorite restaurant, because they allow dogs at their outside tables.

But the boss is already shaking his head. "Too far. I'm beat. Let's grab something from Nancy's and eat it at home. Oh. And I have to stop by the store and get some tomatoes for tomorrow. I think we have everything else." He sighs. "Thought I'd be home earlier when I invited the Franklins."

The Franklins! I forgot! The boss invited them for dinner, because, as I heard him tell Molly, he needs to pay them back for all the times he and Molly have eaten over there. "The score is the Franklins about a zillion, us zero," he said, which I'll admit I didn't understand, since I thought he was talking about dinner and not a game.

Molly says, "You could call and make it another time."

Another shake of the head. "I don't want to postpone it. It'll be fine. I'm just tired."

I wait in the van while the boss and Molly run into the grocery store, and then we pick up some burgers at Nancy's, a fragrant little fast food place a few blocks from our place. I've never been inside since the boss only uses the drive-through.

By the time we pull into our driveway, the whole van smells like burgers and fries.

During dinner, the boss tells Molly how the project went at Miguel's, which could be summarized as Not Well. Sadly, the boss doesn't summarize it, but goes into great detail about delayed deliveries and workmen who didn't show up, and everything taking longer than planned.

"We're now a half a day behind schedule," he says. "So Annie's not sure she can come tomorrow after all, because she may need to stay and help Miguel." He dips a fry in ketchup, and chews a moment in silence. "So, how'd it go with you? Did they have a good crowd?"

Molly, who's been listening a little glaze-eyed, straightens up. "Yeah. I didn't hear how many, but it was a big crowd."

"And her speech? Did she tell everyone how to save the world?"

Molly blinks at this, maybe because of the sudden bitterness in the boss's tone. "She gave a good speech," she says at last. She bites her lip and leans forward, opening her mouth as if to say something more, then shuts it again. She drops her eyes to her plate.

"Sorry," the boss says in a softer voice. "I'm glad it went well. Just not my kind of thing, all that preaching to the choir."

There was a choir there? Funny, I didn't notice.

They finish their burgers in silence, both glum-faced and lost in their own thoughts.

My dinner, after they're done, includes some of Molly's fries and a tiny piece of her burger. Molly puts me outside to pee and to make sure the yard is safe from intruders. When I bark to be let back in, the boss is the one who opens the door.

I find Molly at her desk leaning close to her monitor. "See that?" she tells me, getting up to close the door after I've nosed her hand in greeting. I peer at the screen. A group of people on are standing on some grass—hey, it's the dog fair park. She presses a key that makes it bigger, until all that is showing is someone's legs and feet.

"Can you see it?" she asks.

I'm afraid that I can't. I mean I *see* it, but don't know anything about it. Feet and legs and no trace of a human scent. I sit beside her, thinking another nap might be a good idea.

"I know who stole Hershey," she announces. For some reason, this makes her sad, and she broods about it, staring vacantly at her screen for some time. "Do I tell Mom?" she asks me at one point.

I tilt my head, not knowing what she wants, since she knows I can't possibly answer the question. When she doesn't say anything more, I curl down on the rug.

At one point, she calls Armando, and talks to him and Mariela, but I don't think she mentions Hershey. At least, until I doze off, they are talking about the demonstration, and how great Silvia was—though Molly admits, her voice hesitant with embarrassment, that she didn't hear all of Silvia's speech. The last thing I remember is her apologizing for not being able to see Armando and Mariela before they left.

I wake up to the sound of a click and the TV. Hey, Molly's door is open. I follow her into the living room, where she plops down on the couch beside the boss, who's watching a basketball game. I settle down on my bed, my favorite place because it is so soft.

"Hey, Dad," Molly says, twisting a strand of hair, "I have a problem."

The boss picks up the remote and presses a button, and suddenly the TV goes quiet, always a good thing in my opinion, and then, after a glance at Molly's face, her lips drawn and her eyebrows skewed in worry, presses it again and the TV goes dark. Even better.

"Did . . . did . . ." Molly's frown deepens. "Did Madison tell you Hailey got Hershey back?"

"No," the boss says, clearly surprised. "How'd that happen?"

"Well . . ." Molly launches into the account of how she ran into Hailey at the park. Like the boss earlier, she goes into a lot of detail, telling him all about Hailey and Dominga and the ransom call, so that this turns out to be a very long story. I awake to the boss exclaiming, "I can't believe Madison let you go off by yourself!"

I raise my head to see him flushed with anger.

Molly, her fingers working furiously on a strand of hair, says, "I wasn't by myself. I was with Grady and Hailey."

"Hailey," the boss snorts, shaking his head.

"And Doodle was with me. Anyway, you can't blame her. She didn't know. We, um . . . we did it on our own. And she was plenty mad at us when she found out."

The boss gives Molly a sour look, not speaking, then, studying her face, takes a deep breath and lets it out slowly. "We can talk about that later. The important thing, I guess, is that you're safe. And, I guess, that Hailey got her dog back." He reaches his hand over and rests it on her arm. Then, quietly, "So, you said you had a problem?"

Molly nods. "Yeah. I think I know who took him. And no one will be happy about it." She starts to tell him about the photos she took at the dog fest, after the paint bombs, and somehow I drift off again. I wake up as the boss lets out a big sigh, his eyes dark with sympathy. "I think," he says after a few moments, "that you need to tell your mother about this. She'll know how best to handle it."

"I know," Molly says glumly. "But, what if—"

The boss's phone buzzes. "Annie," he says, his face lighting up. Then he glances at Molly. "Is it okay? She said she'd let me know about tomorrow."

"Sure." Molly sits perched on the couch for a few moments, while the boss talks to Annie. Then she gets up and heads for her room.

Molly has barely closed the door behind us, when her phone starts to buzz. She checks the screen and frowns. "Why is Hailey . . . ?" she mutters, swiping the screen. "Hey."

"Oh, Molly, glad I got you." Hailey's voice comes through the phone as intense as ever. "I need to ask you a really, really big favor. You know how your cousin Silvia does all that immigration stuff?"

"Not really my cousin—" Molly begins.

"But you know her and she'd listen to you?"

"Well . . . maybe . . ."

"Here's the thing. I really need to see Dominga one last time. I didn't even get to say goodbye, you know?" Hailey's voice thickens and I can hear her sniffling. "I didn't even get to say *goodbye*. That's not right."

"Yeah, it sucks," Molly agrees, her voice cautious.

"So, I was thinking maybe Silvia could talk to her and ask Dominga meet me one last time, just for a few minutes. I could be walking Hershey at the park and maybe she could be there just for a few minutes." Another catch in her voice. "Maybe Dominga will listen to Silvia because she's not connected with my family and she understands her situation, you know?"

Hailey pauses and then says in a low, miserable voice, "She won't answer my calls." Another pause. "I think she's afraid my parents won't give her a good recommendation if she sees me. They'd do that, you know? They're mean enough to do that. But if it was all accidental like at the park . . ."

Molly's frown deepens. "I'm not sure . . ."

"Could you at least ask? Because if I can't even say *goodbye*, how am I ever going to—" Hailey's voice breaks and now the sniffling turns to sobs.

Molly sucks in her breath. "I . . . I don't know Silvia that well . . ."

"But could you try?" Hailey seems to be having trouble getting the words out. "Please?"

Molly sighs. "Okay, I guess. I'll . . . try to call."

"Thank you!" Hailey gushes. "Thank you so *so* much."

Molly says goodbye, scrunching her eyes shut for a moment. She takes a deep breath, heaves it out, and picks up her phone, but she doesn't call Silvia. She calls her mother.

"Hey, Mom," she says, starting to twist a strand of hair. "I need to talk to you about something." She recites the whole story of the day in the park. Have I ever mentioned that humans like to repeat themselves?

When, at last, Molly finishes, Cori asks, her voice incredulous, "This guy just returned the dog?"

"Well, no. This is the, um, tricky part." Molly swallows, and takes a deep breath. "If you know someone committed a crime but before they're caught they pay it all back and no one is hurt, would you have to arrest that person?"

Cori doesn't answer immediately. "What do you mean by 'know'? If I have hard evidence that the person is guilty, and their actions hurt someone, probably yes. At least, I'd feel that's what I ought to do."

"What if it's a kid? Who tried to make it right?"

"Well . . ." Cori pauses, then in a gentler voice says, "Molly, why don't you just tell me what happened?"

Molly starts in on the story of how the Hershey ran into the intersection and I think I doze off because the next thing I hear is Cori saying, "The sooner the better. The money might already be spent. Your father's okay with it?"

"If I'm with you and not by myself. And we don't take too long, 'cause the Franklins are coming for dinner and I have to help."

"Cori says. "I have the phone numbers in my interview notes from that DogDays thing. Let me talk to them and call you back."

Molly's face relaxes. She does some texting and after that she calls Tanya. They talk about a bunch of things—never any shortage of conversation with those two—and then Molly says "Grady's going to come over, too, if his mom will drop him off. She has to interview some business guy who says his only free time is Sunday afternoon, so Grady would either be home by himself or have to go with her."

"That'll be great," Tanya says, and then she starts to talk about a homework assignment.

Molly texts Grady after she finishes talking to Tanya. They end up texting a lot. So much so, that Molly has to wake me up to go out for my evening pee. At first, I think something is happening because her voice is more excited than normal. But, no, we go out to the backyard as usual. Well, as usual except Molly's not usually keeping her eyes on her phone. It beeps while I'm finishing my tour of the fence.

"Grady can't make it," she says when I come back to her. "But he knows. He figured it out, just like me, only he didn't have the photos."

Chapter 24

Confrontation

CAN WE TAKE DOODLE?" MOLLY ASKS, STANDING IN
the doorway holding my no-pull harness and a folder of
papers she put together the night before. "He loves to go to the
park." Cori has come to pick her up for the big meeting that she
was on the phone about all evening.

Cori casts a doubtful glance at her car.

"He's clean," Molly says. "Just got groomed a few weeks ago."

"I guess," Cori says, her eyes softening at Molly's eager face.

So I hop into the back seat of her car, not a van like the one
we have, but a sedan, and before long we're pulling into a parking lot. Hey, it's the dog days place. Not many cars here today,
though, and, as Molly puts on my leash and we walk down the
path to the picnic table area, I don't see a single booth or food
tent. A few joggers pass us, and ahead a couple of boys, one of
them with a soccer ball, jostle each other as they hurry down
the path. But otherwise, the park is empty.

We stop at one of the picnic tables, and Molly and Cori sit
down. I have to say I'm disappointed, because it's a great day
for a walk. The sun is warm and the air is still and heavy with

scents of growing things and the buzzing of insects. Squirrel scents, too, although not nearly as many as in the park with all the statues.

"I put the photos on this," Cori says, handing Molly a tablet—not the paper kind but those things called tablets that are like small computers. While Molly swipes at the tablet's screen, I glean a couple of fries and a crust of ketchup-encrusted bun from underneath the table. Molly taps her foot nervously. She's as jumpy as a horse on a windy day and has been ever since she got up. Not sure why.

What Molly needs is to get up from this table and take a walk, like that man and his border collie I see crossing the park. Take it from me, you will *always* feel better after a walk. I give Molly a nudge with my nose, but she ignores it.

Then Molly sucks in her breath. "There they are," she says.

I don't recognize the approaching figures at first, but as they get closer I see it is Dominga and a boy walking beside her, his shoulders slumped, head down.

They come up to the picnic bench and sink down on the bench across from Molly and Cori without a word. Something about the boy looks—no, smells—familiar. I sniff discretely, trying to figure it out. And then the scent triggers a memory: the boy in the hooded sweatshirt throwing the leash at Molly. He looks much thinner in just a plain T-shirt. Much younger. Just a kid.

"Thank you for coming," Cori says in that polite but firm voice cops often have. "I'm not sure if you've met my daughter, Molly?"

Dominga, scents of fear clinging to her, gives Molly a nod and a fleeting smile. Little beads of sweat shine on her forehead.

The boy stares at the table, his face sullen. Cori says, "And you're Mario? I met your mother at the DogDays thing last week, but not you."

Mario shrugs.

"You already know I'm a cop. But . . ." Cori hesitates, and glances at Molly, whose eyes are fixed on her mother's face, then turns back at Dominga. "But I understand your situation. My parents came here from Mexico and lived here many years before they were—" her voice hardens "—deported. When they left, I chose to stay. It was—" she closes her eyes for a second "—a very hard decision. They still live in Mexico and I haven't seen them in years. It has caused a lot . . . of problems." Cori clears her throat. "I'm telling you this so you know I understand some of what you have to go through as an immigrant. So you won't be afraid of me."

"Were your parents risking death by going back to their country?" Dominga asks in a harsh voice.

Cori seems taken aback. "No," she admits.

"You are lucky they live in Mexico and not El Salvador." Neither speak for a moment. Finally, Dominga says, "But I'm okay. I have a work permit. I'm not illegal."

"Good." Cori flashes a brief smile. "Although I wouldn't care if you were, not for why we are here today." In her all-business voice, she continues. "Molly called me yesterday to say she knew who stole Hailey's dog, but she thought maybe we could work things out so no one has to be arrested."

"Because you saved Hershey," Molly blurts, looking at Mario. "You could have left him to get hit by a car, but you didn't."

For a moment, Mario stares at her, speechless. "You have no proof," he says at last. His voice, belligerent, reminds me of a

Chihuahua barking at a larger dog. "No one could recognize the people there."

Cori, regarding him with pity, says softly, "And how could you possibly know that?"

Mario clamps his mouth shut, suddenly looking very young and very scared.

"*This* is why you asked us to come here?" Dominga gives Cori an indignant look, and then regards her son with a mixture of alarm and sadness. "*You* took that dog?"

Mario stares at the table.

"But you weren't even at the park that day! Until later, after the dog had been taken."

"He was there," Molly says, "He just made sure you didn't see him. Right, Mario?"

He meets Molly's gaze, his own eyes angry. "You have no proof."

"I'm afraid Molly does have proof," Cori says gently, "at least that you were the one who returned him." She gestures at the tablet in front of her daughter. "Molly?"

Molly swipes the screen and slides it across the table. "I have a shot of you and your mother at the dog fair," she says. She angles the tablet so he can see it. "And this is the same thing zoomed in," she says tapping the screen again. "See the shoes? And this—" another tap "—is the shoes of the boy who threw Hershey's leash to me."

Mario's gaze shifts to his feet, to the bright shoes that are higher in the front than at the heel, and then back up again. "Lots of people have these shoes," he says, still the Chihuahua fending off the intruder.

"Not with fluorescent blue and orange laces," Molly says.

"Those shoes!" Dominga looks from the tablet to her son, and back to the tablet. "He loves those shoes. Too much money, I told him. But he worked for a neighbor and saved up for months to help pay for them"

"Stupid dog. Stupid, *stupid* dog!" Mario says in a savage voice. "We had it all planned perfectly. No one would know."

"But you saved him," Molly says. "If you hadn't gone back for him, he probably would have gotten hit."

"I couldn't let him die. Even though that stupid Hailey doesn't deserve him." Now his eyes fill with tears. "Stupid dog."

"Supid *boy*!" Dominga's words are clipped with anger. "Why would you do such a thing? Risk everything I've worked so hard so we could live here, so you could have a chance at a better life—"

"You work all the time, night and day," Mario retorts. "All the time for that family, never any time for your own family, only that stupid girl and then they fire you just like that!" He snaps his fingers. "That's how much you mean to them. Why shouldn't they have to pay us a little more? They don't care about you, about us. But all you seem to care about is that girl."

For a moment, no one speaks.

"It was my job," Dominga says. "I care for her because that's how I care for you."

Mario waves his hand as if brushing away flies.

Dominga slaps her hand on the table, making Mario jump. "You are why I do *everything*. If you don't understand that, you are the stupid one." She changes into Spanish, a rush of words with lots of hand gestures and Mario responds. Cori listens with interest. As I might have mentioned before, my Spanish is mostly limited to foods, but it doesn't take a translator to hear the pain and anger in their voices. When the exchange is finally done, they both look exhausted and sad.

A long silence follows.

Finally, Cori turns to Mario. "Who were you working with?"

Mario, his eyes on the table, says, "Just a friend. I . . . I don't want to get him in trouble. His brother had a car so we could get the dog to the park."

In a low voice, Dominga resumes talking in Spanish, a series of questions by her tone. Then she stops abruptly, looking at Cori.

"I know who," Dominga says. "But do you have to—?"

"Here's what I'm thinking," Cori says. "Mario, look at me." Mario reluctantly meets her gaze. "If you and your friend, who we'll keep nameless, will return the money, we'll let the matter drop. Will you do that?"

Mario says in a defeated voice, all his anger gone now, "I guess. I have it all except . . . we had to pay Ri—I mean my friend's brother twenty-five dollars. For driving—oh, and ten dollars for dogfood."

"I'll pay that part," Dominga says, and, with a stern look at her son, "And you will earn every penny of it and pay me back."

Mario nods mutely.

For a few minutes no one speaks. Mario's head is bent toward the table. Dominga looks straight ahead, her eyes unfocused. Molly, biting her lower lip, looks from her mother to Dominga.

And then a voice breaks the silence, one, unfortunately, that I'd recognize anywhere. "Dominga!"

Dominga sucks in her breath as we all turn to watch Hailey hurrying down the path towards us, Hershey in front of her tugging on the leash.

"What is *she* doing here?" Dominga asks angrily.

Molly, her face flushed, begins talking so fast her words seem to fall on one another. "I was going to tell you but we ran out of time. I told her to come. That you'd be here. She just really needs a chance to say goodbye. She won't tell her parents because she knows you need them to give you a good rec. But she *really* needs this, so I told her we'd be here today . . ." the words end and her voice trails off.

Cori is frowning at Molly. Mario makes a disgusted sound and stands up. "I don't want to see her," he says.

"She doesn't know anything about Hershey. About you," Molly says quickly. "And we won't ever tell her. She just wants to say goodbye to your mom. For just a couple of minutes?" She turns to Dominga, her eyes pleading.

When Hailey finally reaches us, Hershey suddenly starts barking, lunging at the end of the leash toward Mario.

"Hey, thanks for doing this," she says, a little breathlessly to Molly. She holds the leash out to Mario.

"Could you hold him for me?" she asks. "Just for a minute?"

Mario hesitates for a second and then takes the leash. Hershey jumps up on him, ecstatic with his greeting.

"Can we—" Hailey gives Dominga a searing look, waving a hand toward the other picnic tables "—talk in private? *Really* short, I promise."

Dominga, stone-faced, rises and slowly follows Hailey. Hershey doesn't seem to know she's gone, all his attention on Mario.

"I think that dog prefers you to his owner," Cori says to Mario.

Well, yeah. Just look at him. Hershey's whole backend is swaying along with his tail, the same way Snippet does with Grady.

Mario bends down to scratch Hershey's ears. "He's always liked me. That's why he went with me." His voice becomes very soft. "I like him, too. I wish . . . We can't have dogs where we live. Ri—um, my friend had to keep him . . ." He doesn't say anything more but stares morosely ahead, his face as sad as a hound's.

In the distance, Hailey and Dominga are talking. Well, mostly Hailey, her arms flying through the air in her typical big gestures, the way they always do when she's speaking. She talks for some time, then rushes forward and flings her arms around Dominga in a fierce hug. When she releases her nanny, she turns and practically runs back to us.

"Thanks!" Hailey whispers, her eyes wet and swollen. She grabs Hershey's leash and marches resolutely toward the parking lot. Mario stares after her, arms at his side, not moving.

Dominga following more slowly, comes back to the table and stands stiffly beside it, her face expressionless.

Hailey never looks back. Hershey, however, lags behind, turning to look at Mario, until Hailey jerks the leash and he catches up.

No one speaks until Hailey has disappeared from view. Then Cori rises, clears her throat again and says to Dominga, "Can I come by your home to get the money?"

"Yes." They start to talk about what time would be convenient, but just then Molly rises and I think maybe we'll get our walk after all. I jump up, ready to go.

No such luck. With a terse goodbye, Dominga starts back for the parking lot, Mario's thin, slump-shouldered figure by her side.

"I'll get you home." For some reason, Cori sounds angry when she says this, and, whoa, suddenly tension pours from Molly, my nose twitching as I take in the scent.

Cori sets a brisk pace, and neither she nor Molly speak until we're almost to the car.

"I don't like being blindsided," Cori says in a cold voice. "Hailey . . ."

Molly's grip tightens on the leash. "She begged me. And I was afraid you'd say no. She really needed to say goodbye. So she can get over it. Dominga was like a mother to her—at least Hailey thinks that even though Dominga doesn't—and to have her disappear without even saying goodbye . . ." Molly stops speaking, her eyes suddenly widening with dismay.

"Like I did?" Cori asks, her voice harsh.

"I didn't mean—I didn't think—I really didn't mean—" Tears well in Molly's eyes. "I didn't think . . ." I press my nose to Molly's hand but she doesn't seem to notice.

Cori stares at her for a second, then pulls her into a short, awkward hug. "It's okay. Never mind. Let's just get you home."

We get to the car and Molly loads me into the back seat. She's leaning in to unsnap the leash when I look up just as Cori opens the driver-side door. Whoa. Now Cori's cheeks are wet with tears. Molly gives a tiny gasp when she sees her mother, as she straightens up to shut the door. But she says nothing, and neither of them speaks the whole way home.

I have to admit that I'm glad when Cori pulls into our driveway. I've been to a lot of parks in my life, but I don't remember a single trip that has ever been this sad.

I think it's because we never got that walk.

Chapter 25

Happier Times

WHEN WE GET HOME, THE HOUSE SMELLS MARVEL-ous! Not just the taco meat and beans, which are won-derful, but another scent I'm always happy to smell. Annie! I wonder if she brought another bone.

As soon as we're inside, Annie rushes over to us. Once again her hair is down, and she is wearing a shiny blouse and slacks instead of her usual T-shirt and jeans. She hugs Molly.

"You made it!" Molly exclaims, happier than she's been all day.

"Couldn't miss it. I hear we're getting *frijoles supremos*," Annie says, laughing.

"Armando's recipe." Molly beams at her, nodding. "From his restaurant."

The boss emerges from the bathroom, holding a toilet bowl brush, his hands encased in rubber gloves. "How'd it go?" he asks Molly.

Molly only hesitates a second. "Good. They worked it all out."

He studies her a moment, and then smiles. "Good. Can you start cutting up the salad stuff?"

"Sure!" She heads for the kitchen.

"And you, Mr. Doodle," Annie says, scratching me under my chin in that way I particularly like, "have a playdate in the backyard."

That can only mean one thing. Annie brought her beagle, Chloe, which is even better than a bone because Chloe and I are best buds. I smelled Chloe's scent all over her, of course, but Annie always carries Chloe's scent on her. I follow Annie to the backdoor, and soon Chloe and I are chasing each other from one end of the yard to the other. Which, admittedly, is not very great distance, but it's good enough for a romp.

We hear the Franklin's van pull into the driveway after a while, and rush to the fence to bark a little before going back to our game. Is this a great night or what?

Finally, we stop and lap long drinks from the water bowl by the door before flopping on the ground in exhaustion. After we've rested a bit, we sniff out the perimeter of the fence, peeing every place we need to leave our scent.

Speaking of scents, I catch a whiff of the taco meat and suddenly realize that I'm outside and the food is inside. I go to the door and bark. No response. I bark again. Still no response. I let out a loud volley of barks, and Chloe, catching the spirit, howls.

The door flies open. "Good grief, Doodle," Molly says, looking exasperated. "Hurry. It's already started."

Chloe and I follow her through the kitchen, where plastic plates with bits of food on them are stacked on the table—looks like we've missed dinner—and into the living room. Chloe rushes over to Annie to get a pat, and then—hey!—lies down on my bed. What the—?

Mr. Franklin, thin and white-capped, sits next to Mrs. Franklin's broad form on the couch, his hand resting on her arm. The boss sits at the far end of the couch, next to the chair where Annie is. Tanya and Tyson are sitting on chairs that have been moved in from the kitchen. Molly takes a seat on the boss's desk chair that has been pulled next to Tanya's. I don't see the older Franklin boys, but that doesn't surprise me. They're always off doing sports.

I sink down onto my bed, half on top of Chloe so she has to scoot over and give me the middle. Much better.

Everyone is staring at the TV, at Madison, frozen in place, her eyes brimming with sincerity. Behind her, Mariela holds a tearful Tony. The boss clicks the remote and she starts to move. Suddenly, the sound blares out so loudly that everyone jumps, myself included. "Sorry!" the boss calls out. "Hit the wrong thing." He fiddles with the remote until the sound gets softer.

"—a happy ending to our good-news story of the week," Madison says, a big smile on her face.

Then the smile fades and Madison leans forward, her face now serious. The screen changes to one of Suzanne and Jason at the back of the HEAR van, both looking angry.

"Molly's photo," Tanya says with excitement.

Madison's voice becomes somber. "A source from the Arlington Police Department confirmed today that two suspects have been taken in for questioning, and search warrants had been issued for several vehicles belonging to the organization Humans for Enlightened Animal Relations, or HEAR. This is after Thursday's *Low Down News* aired photos taken in an Arlington neighborhood showing possible evidence linking HEAR to the paint-bombs at the Arlington DogDays last week."

A photo of a park appears on the screen. "You can see the two HEAR employees at the DogDays here—" a black arrow suddenly appears right over the head of a boy in a baseball cap "—and here." Another arrow points to the head of a girl on the other side of the arena. "These same employees have been seen in a HEAR van in an Arlington neighborhood where several beloved pets recently disappeared." The screen switches back to the photo of the two behind the HEAR van.

"Jason and Suzanne," Molly says. "But I didn't recognize Suzanne when we first met her, because you can't really tell who they are in the photo without blowing it up."

Something's going to blow up? I watch with interest, but nothing happens except Madison's face fills the screen again.

"That's right, folks. You heard it here on the *Low Down News* first. Thanks to two intrepid dog-loving reporters—" she smiles at the camera and both Molly and Tanya giggle "—who prefer to remain unnamed, the police are now investigating HEAR for both the Arlington DogDays paint bombings, and the disappearance of pets in several Arlington neighborhoods."

"So the police arrested Suzanne and Jason?" Tanya asks. "Is that what 'taken in for questioning' means?"

"I don't think 'taken in for questioning' means arrested," Mr. Franklin says in his deep voice. "But it can lead to an arrest."

Tanya turns to Molly. "Did your mom tell you she was taking them in?"

Molly shakes her head. "She can't talk about work like that. Has to keep it confidential. But—" Molly smiles briefly "—she told me my photos helped them get search warrants." She looks back up at the screen, where a man with the big glasses is standing in front of a building.

"—spokesman denies all responsibility on the part of HEAR," the man intones. "We do not condone nor advocate any illegal activity, and if these alleged accusations prove to be true, they are the work of individuals working entirely on their own, explicitly against company policy."

Madison says, "And in other news . . ." and the boss clicks off the T.V.

Mrs. Franklin shakes her head in disgust. "So they're scapegoating the employees. Typical. And they look like they're just kids."

"They're not kids," Tanya retorts. "Remember, they killed Dan. They ought to toss those two in jail and throw away the key."

For a moment, no one speaks.

"Do you think it really was just Suzanne and Jason acting on their own?" Molly asks.

The boss snorts. "I think HEAR has enough lawyers to pass the buck."

Annie nods in agreement. "I wouldn't be surprised if it's not the company's unofficial policy to let their employees do what they want to further the cause, but if they get caught, they're on their own."

"There's a lot of that goin' around," Mrs. Franklin says. "See it all the time at work. Don't do this—nudge, nudge, wink, wink."

While I'm trying to figure out what that means, Tanya asks, "What's intrepid?" She grins. "Sure hope Madison wasn't calling us ugly!"

"Fearless," Annie says, smiling. "Adventurous."

"Skating on the edge of restriction." Mrs. Franklin fixes Tanya with a warning stare, and Tanya drops her eyes to her feet.

"So we're intrepid and unnamed," Molly says. "I can live with that."

"How many photos did she use?" Tanya asks. "Of yours, I mean."

Molly smiles. "Six! Madison told me she'll pay me $150! She turns to Tanya. "I'm sharing it with you, because if you hadn't been talking to Jason and Suzanne, I could have never gotten the photos. Plus, you were the one who found Mr. Williams. And saved my camera!"

Tanya's face lights up at this, but Mrs. Franklin frowns. "I hope this doesn't inspire you to become more *intrepid*," she says, narrowing her eyes at her daughter.

Mr. Franklin smiles at both girls. "I think you two did good work. Even if HEAR weasels out of the charges, just the fact that the police are questioning them ought to slow them down a bit."

"Now don't you go encouraging them," Mrs. Franklin says. But her mouth creases into a smile as she rises and walks into the kitchen.

She comes back holding a large plate full of cookies and a stack of napkins. "Oatmeal or chocolate chip," she says, offering napkins and cookies to everyone in the room, except, of course, us dogs.

The boss reaches for several of each kind. "I'm glad you insisted on bringing dessert," he says with enthusiasm.

"No oatmeal for me," Tanya says, taking a small handful when the plate comes her way. She holds up one of the cookies, examining it. "Hershey!" she says, as if suddenly remembering something. "Did HEAR people steal him, too? If so, why would they give him back?"

Molly and the boss exchange a glance.

"Hailey doesn't know who stole him." Molly starts to twist a strand of hair. "Probably wasn't HEAR or he wouldn't still be alive. She's just grateful she got him back."

Chloe moves off my bed to go sit in front of Annie, staring mournfully up at her. Annie laughs, rising from her chair. "That's my signal that it's time to feed these critters," she says.

We follow her to the kitchen. Besides our kibble, we get a little of leftover meat that Annie scrapes from the paper plates before throwing them in the trash. A little bit of lettuce, too, but I leave that in my dish. I'm a dog, not a rabbit.

By the time we finish eating, go out for another pee, and come back in, the Franklins are at the door, gushing about how great the dinner was and thanking the boss for having them over.

"And you said you couldn't cook," Mrs. Franklin says, shaking her head.

"Nothing but salad," the boss replies. "If it's salad, I'm not too bad."

They say their goodbyes and leave, and then Annie gathers up hers and Chloe's things.

"Thanks for all the help." The boss pulls Annie into a long hug. "Thanks," he repeats in a low voice. Molly watches, relaxed and grinning.

Later, after the boss and Molly have cleaned up the dishes, which turns out to be mostly throwing away all the paper plates and cups, they drag the chairs back to the kitchen, and then turn out the light, and go into the living room. I settle down on my bed.

"I think that went well," the boss says, rolling his office chair, the only one left, to his bedroom. "Our first dinner party."

"Yeah," Molly agrees. Her eyes are on her phone, which keeps giving text beeps.

"Who's that?" the boss asks.

"Grady." She hesitates. "He figured out that Mario was the one who stole Hershey. Recognized the shoes. Like I did, only he didn't have the photos."

"Smart kid," the boss says.

"He was wondering how everything went, with Mom talking to Mario and everything, so I let him know."

The boss picks up the remote, turning it in his hand. "I was going to ask about that. You seemed a little down when you came home. How did it go?"

Molly's lips tighten. "It was . . . hard," she says. "Mario is jealous of Hailey, and angry that her folks just fired his mom. And, I think he really likes Hershey. I think it was hard for him to give him back. So that was sad, and then Hailey came to say goodbye to Dominga and that was really sad."

"Hailey showed up?" The boss tilts his head in surprise. He sets down the remote. "How'd she know about it?"

Molly's gaze is fixed on her lap. "Um . . . well . . . I told her. She called me and was really upset about not getting to say goodbye and I just thought . . . thought she should have a chance. You know?"

"Yeah." The boss gives Molly a sad look, his eyes full of understanding. "I know."

"I feel sorry for her," Molly says. "I mean, Mom wasn't . . . around when I was little, but I always had you, and when you were working, I had Marmie and GrandJum. I always had family. You didn't hire a bunch of nannies and then fire them whenever I started to like them." She scrunches her eyes shut and when she opens them, they're wet with tears. "I always had you, a real parent. Not like poor Hailey, who doesn't have anyone who really loves her."

"Oh, Molly," the boss says. He swoops her up high, and then holds her close. "You will *always* have me," he says, his voice thick with emotion.

Molly mumbles something I can't understand except for the word "family."

Family? Hey! What about me? I jump off my bed and run over and lean against them. For some reason, this makes them both laugh.

"Oh, Doodle. You don't want to be left out." Molly pulls away just enough that I can stick my head in the gap between her and the boss.

"Group hug," she says happily.

And, despite the fact that both she and the boss have tears in their eyes, the scent of joy and of contentment flows from them with such intensity that before I know it, a couple of resounding barks burst from me.

"Oh, Doodle," Molly says, laughing again.

"Trust Doodle to ruin the moment," the boss says, but he's also laughing as he sets Molly down and bends to give me an affectionate scratch under the chin.

Ruin the moment? Not at all sure what he means, but it doesn't matter. I go over to my bed and curl down on it.

Everyone is happy and that's good enough for me.

Chapter 26

Moving On

TODAY, IT'S SO WARM THAT EVEN IN THE SHADE OF Mrs. Carter's porch, I'm panting a little. The boss said earlier that the weather report states this will be the warmest first week in April on record.

Molly and Tanya, seated on folding chairs, are both in bright shorts and sleeveless tops. Mrs. Carter, reclines in one of those padded rockers that she's moved to the porch since we were last here, beside a round table that holds a plastic pitcher of lemonade and some paper cups. She dabs at beads of sweat on her forehead with a crinkly handkerchief that has a sharp, perfumy smell. We're waiting for Annie, who, according to Molly, should be here any minute.

"At first, I said no," Mrs. Carter is telling the girls. "I loved Dan so much—" her eyes get a bit watery, but she dabs them with handkerchief as well "—I said I just couldn't have another dog." She purses her lips for a moment and presses the handkerchief to her forehead before continuing.

"She told me she knows how it's always hard to lose a dog. 'They're part of your family,'" she said. 'I understand. It's hard for dogs, too.' But then she told me she had a dog who had belonged to an elderly lady who recently passed away. 'She's sweet, well-behaved, and right now she's feeling as lonely for her owner as you are for Dan,' she said. 'Dogs grieve just like we do when they lose someone they love, but the great thing about dogs is that they are almost always ready to open their hearts to someone new. They don't dwell on the past, but move on.'"

Mrs. Carter scrunches her handkerchief in her hand. "She told me she thought this dog might be perfect for me." She presses the cloth to her forehead. "I said I just wasn't sure I was ready. But that Annie is a wise woman. So nice, you know?"

Both Molly and Tanya nod. They've heard this story before, from Annie, and they talked about it when we walked over, but they listen politely.

"She told me if we close our hearts every time we lose someone we love, pretty soon there'll be nothing inside us but an empty shell. That's what she said." Mrs. Carter shuts her eyes for a second, then turns to look directly at the girls. "And then she said, 'Just meet this dog and see how it goes. If you like her, you can keep her, and if you decide she's not the dog for you, then I'll take her back and find a good home for her.' So," Mrs. Carter lets out a long sigh, "I said I'd at least meet the dog. Would you like some more lemonade?"

Molly glances at her cup, still half full, on the table and shakes her head. Tanya says, "Yes, please," and Mrs. Carter refills her cup.

And then I sit up as I hear Annie's van turn the corner.

She parks along the curb, gets out, opens the backend, connects a leash and lifts out a fluffy, cream-colored dog that's about the size of a beagle, but shaped more like a small spaniel.

She sets the dog on the ground and walks up to us, the dog trotting smartly by her side.

Mrs. Carter hefts herself out of the rocker, and smiles at Annie and the dog as they come up the steps, and then join us on the porch.

"Oh, she's cute," Tanya says.

"Meet Wanda," Annie says. "She's a Shih Tzu/Cavalier King's Spaniel/who-knows-what-else mix. She has the sweet temperament of a Cavalier, and more of a Cavalier coat as well."

"Well, how do you do Miss Wanda?" Mrs. Carter says, bending with some effort to stroke her head. "You're a pretty little thing."

Molly and Tanya pet her, marveling over the softness of her coat. Wanda stands calmly throughout, and remains calm when it's my turn to greet her. Some small dogs get nervous around me, because of my size, but, as we sniff noses and butts, Wanda is confident and friendly. She could be a Canine Good Citizen.

Mrs. Carter waves at a folding chair. "Have a seat. Would you like some lemonade?"

Annie, smiling, says, "Sure. I can pour it myself."

Mrs. Carter sinks down into her chair, with a little sigh of relief. "She certainly is well-behaved," she says to Annie, then leans toward the dog and says, "Aren't you, Miss Wanda?"

Wanda goes over to Mrs. Carter, sits, tilts her head, and stares directly into Mrs. Carter's eyes, all the time working her nose. Then, suddenly, with a short little bark, she leaps up onto Mrs. Carter's lap, curls down, and starts to lick her hand.

"Oh!" exclaim Annie and Mrs. Carter at the same time, clearly surprised.

"She must like you." Annie starts to tug on the leash. "Wanda—"

"Oh, leave her," Mrs. Carter says, stroking Wanda's silky coat. "She's fine right here." Her gaze returns to Wanda. "Aren't you the softest dog I've ever petted?" Wanda gives her hand a few more licks.

"She'll shed some," Annie says, "and you'll need to keep her coat brushed out. I can give you the names of some groomers if—"

"We know a good groomer," Molly offers. "Mrs. Yashimoto. She does Doodle and she's great."

Annie says, "I brought a bag of the dog food she's been eating, to get you started, and—" she glances at Molly and Tanya.

"We bought a harness and leash for her," Tanya says, handing Mrs. Carter a brightly colored bag. "Molly and me. We wanted to do something, because we were so sorry about Dan."

"Why . . ." Mrs. Carter presses her handkerchief to her eyes. "Thank you," she says, taking the bag and peering into it. "I don't know what to say."

Annie says, "Like I told you earlier, if you feel at any time that she's not the dog for you, just call me and I'll come and get her. I won't mind a bit. I don't want you to feel obligated to keep her if you don't really want to."

It's hard to tell if Mrs. Carter is listening. Her eyes are still on Wanda, and she's murmuring something to the dog as Annie is talking.

"Here's my card, with all my contact information," Annie rises, holding it out.

Mrs. Carter finally looks up. She takes the card, and studies it a second. "I don't think I'll need this," she says, setting it on the table. She gives Annie a big smile.

"I think Miss Wanda and me are going to be just fine."

About the Author

SUSAN J. KROUPA IS A DOG LOVER CURRENTLY OWNED by a 70-pound labradoodle whose superpower is bringing home dead possums and raccoons. She is also an award-winning author whose fiction has appeared in *Realms of Fantasy,* and in a variety of professional anthologies, including *Bruce Coville's Shapeshifters.* Her non-fiction publications include features about environmental issues and Hopi Indian culture for *The Arizona Republic, High Country News,* and *American Forests.*

She now lives in the Blue Ridge Mountains in Southwest-

ern Virginia, where she's busy writing the next Doodlebugged mystery. You can read her blog at https://www .susankroupa.com.

Authors depend upon reviews and word-of-mouth. It truly makes a difference! If you enjoyed this book, please consider writing a review on Amazon, Barnes & Noble, or any other ebook retailer. It can be as short as a couple of sentences—every review helps and will be greatly appreciated.

Don't Miss Out! Subscribe to Susan's newsletter at http://eepurl.com/3PUR1 and receive a free short story, plus advance notice when new books are published. Your email will never be shared and you can unsubscribe at any time.

Acknowledgements

THANKS, AS ALWAYS, TO MY SON, JOSEPH KROUPA, AN attorney who lives in Arlington, Virginia. Not only is he my patient, go-to Photoshop guru, but he is also my go-to guy for astute legal advice on matters book-related and other. The photos he generously took of Lafayette Square filled in the details I couldn't find on Google Maps alone.

In addition to numerous online sources, Tasha Blaine's book, *Just Like Family: Inside the Lives of Nannies, the Parents They Work for, and the Children They Love,* gave me valuable insights into the issues faced by nannies in the U.S. today.

As in previous books, I owe a debt to Marti Jones. My interviews with her when she was the Executive Director and Senior Staff Attorney at the Immigration Project in Bloomington, Illinois, helped me to create the histories of Cori's family and extended relatives.

Naturally, any errors in the book are my own.

I'm grateful to Sara Hoskinson Frommer, first reader, dear friend, and author of the excellent Joan Spencer mysteries. It is not hyperbole to say that she improves everything I write. As Doodle would say, she saves my bacon.

I am indebted also to Patricia Castelli and Lyn Worthen, both fine writers themselves, for their insight and their keen editorial eye.

And finally, thanks to Tom for his calm, unflinching support when it matters most. He truly is grace under fire.

More Molly & Doodle

BED-BUGGED: *Doodlebugged Mysteries #1*

Ask Doodle why he flunked out of service-dog school and he'll tell you: smart and obedient don't always go hand in hand. Now he has a new job sniffing out bed bugs for his new boss, Josh Hunter. The best part of the job? Molly, the boss's ten-year old daughter, who slips Doodle extra treats when she's not busy snapping photos with her new camera. But Molly has secrets of her own. And when she enlists Doodle's help to solve a crime, his nose and her camera lead them straight to danger. A charming mystery for dog lovers of all ages.

OUT-SNIFFED: *Doodlebugged Mysteries #2*

Doodle's back! The obedience-impaired sniffer dog, who delighted dog lovers and gentle-mystery fans alike in *Bed-Bugged,* returns for another laugh-out-loud adventure.

This time, Doodle's nose gets put to the test when Molly starts training him to find something very different from bed bugs to clear her best friend's brother from drug charges. But when Doodle fails an important certification trial, the boss is furious. Has Molly's extra training has ruined Doodle's ability to do his job?

It takes all of Molly's ingenuity and Doodle's keen intelligence to sniff out what really happened and set things right again.

A nominee for the Maxwell Medallion by the Dog Writers Association of America.

DOG-NABBED: *Doodlebugged Mysteries #3*

What's not to love about a trip the Blue Ridge Mountains? Doodle has a blast—biggest yard *ever,* plus wild turkeys to chase—while Molly enjoys visiting her grandparents. But then Molly's good friend, Lizzie, begs for help. Lizzie's father, under the influence of a self-proclaimed prophet named Zeke, forbids Lizzie to see anyone not approved by Zeke—not Molly, and, worse, not even Lizzie's desperately ill grandmother. Defying Zeke, Molly and Lizzie meet secretly in the woods where a discovery makes Molly think Zeke's hiding something. But how can she prove it?

As for Doodle, he loves all these hikes through the woods. Until he and Molly, hot on Zeke's trail, end up lost—seriously, *not* his fault—and he begins to wonder if they'll ever make it home again.

BAD-MOUTHED: *Doodlebugged Mysteries #4*

Doodle's the first to admit he doesn't get Christmas. His job is to find bedbugs for his boss's bedbug detection business and to watch over the boss's ten-year-old daughter, Molly. It is not to play a black sheep in a Christmas pageant, a lose-lose situation for sure. Not to mention that just when things start to get interesting, Doodle attracts the attention of a popular video-blogger, whose subsequent "feature" jeopardizes the boss's business.

Throw in a handful of threatening letters, a devastating fire and some lost dogs, and Molly and Doodle have their hands— well, in Doodle's case, his paws—full finding out just who's been naughty and who's been nice.

A laugh-out-loud mystery perfect for the any season.

 Visit Laurel Fork Press to learn more about these and upcoming new titles.

www.laurelforkpress.com

68521287R00150